THE WITCH DOLL

Ten-year-old Linda knows from the beginning that there is something strange about the old doll which drops from the back of a rag-and-bone cart, but when Joanna puts on the doll's wig and brushes her hair, Linda's vague uneasiness turns to horror – the doll begins to grow, move and speak. There is no doubt that its intentions are evil, and when Linda learns the doll's history from a friend's grand-mother, it is even more terrifying than she had imagined. Then Joanna is bewitched and Linda re-solves to save her – but in order to do so she must face the possibility of a chilling enchantment. A thrilling story of witchcraft and the supernatural to grip readers from the start.

Helen Morgan was born in 1921 and became a bookworm as soon as she could read. Having lost her sight at the age of twelve, she partially regained it a year later and trained as a shorthand typist at a school for the blind. Always a keen writer, she also liked listening to music, radio and TV plays. She was married with three daughters. Her other books in Puffin are *Meet Mary Kate*, *Mary Kate and the Jumble Bear* and *Mary Kate and the School Bus*. Helen Morgan died in 1990.

Other books by Helen Morgan

MARY KATE AND THE JUMBLE BEAR
MARY KATE AND THE SCHOOL BUS
MEET MARY KATE

The
Witch Doll

Helen Morgan

PUFFIN BOOKS

PUFFIN BOOKS

Published by the Penguin Group
Penguin Books Ltd, 27 Wrights Lane, London w8 5TZ, England
Penguin Books USA Inc., 375 Hudson Street, New York, New York 10014, USA
Penguin Books Australia Ltd, Ringwood, Victoria, Australia
Penguin Books Canada Ltd, 10 Alcorn Avenue, Toronto, Ontario, Canada M4V 3B2
Penguin Books (NZ) Ltd, 182–190 Wairau Road, Auckland 10, New Zealand

Penguin Books Ltd, Registered Offices: Harmondsworth, Middlesex, England

First published by Hamish Hamilton Ltd 1991
Published in Puffin Books 1992
1 3 5 7 9 10 8 6 4 2

Printed in England by Clays Ltd, St Ives plc

For Nansi

Contents

PART ONE
Quay Street: 1987

Chapter One	The Doll	11
Chapter Two	Tilda	21
Chapter Three	Angie	31
Chapter Four	Gran	43

PART TWO
The House on the Esplanade:

1919–1920

Chapter Five	Miss Lucy	57
Chapter Six	The Governess	73
Chapter Seven	Elsie	87
Chapter Eight	Bessie	103

PART THREE
Quay Street: 1987

| Chapter Nine | Time... | 119 |
| Chapter Ten | ... and Tide | 132 |

Quay Street:
1987

CHAPTER ONE

The Doll

Linda sat on the front doorstep, her arms round her knees, her head down. The strong July sun beat on the back of her neck and under her bare feet the cobblestones were hopping hot. She was bored. Her brother had gone fishing and her best friend, Angie, had gone to visit her grandparents and wouldn't be back till the evening.

The quiet of a sleepy summer afternoon hung over the little town. The tiny houses in the short, steep street that led up from the quayside to the ancient castle seemed to be leaning against one another, their rooftops rising step by step to the ruined tower at the top of the hill.

Quay Street was very narrow and knobbly and there were no pavements, but no traffic ever came that way – except old Mr Baldock and his donkey-cart.

Mr Baldock was what Linda's grandmother called 'a rag-and-bone man' but nobody ever offered him rags or bones now. He collected all manner of oddments – old clothes, ornaments, pots and pans, fenders, prams, coal scuttles and sometimes small items of good furniture – anything that would go on his rickety old cart. It was the sound of his cart, clanking and rattling up the hill, that roused Linda from her dreamy doze.

She lifted her head and looked through half-closed eyes down the hill towards the quayside. A white-winged sailing boat bobbed like a bird on the sparkling water behind the donkey-cart that rumbled slowly towards her. Mr Baldock sat, slumped and sleepy after a good lunch in the Dog and Duck, the reins slack in his hands. The donkey knew its way home. Blinkered, it came with lowered head and sure, careful tread towards the step where Linda sat. Mr Baldock did not look up as the little cart passed her. The wheels rattled over the cobblestones only a few inches away from Linda's feet and the cart was fairly crammed with household goods. Mr Baldock had had a good day. The last thing he had put on the cart was a mahogany chest of drawers. It stood upright and securely roped. There were three small drawers at the top – but one of these had escaped the careful criss-crossing of the rope.

As the cart went up the steep slope towards Mr Baldock's yard, one wheel went over a shallow step. When it thumped down again the drawer was jerked out. It fell with a crash to the cobblestones and something flew out of it and landed at Linda's feet.

She picked it up, and shouted, 'Mr Baldock!' with all her might. Then she looked at the thing she was holding. It was an old, embroidered-canvas needlework bag, with wooden handles. There was something hard inside it.

Linda shouted again and opened the bag. It smelled musty. She saw odd scraps of material, a needlecase, and something else. At the bottom of the bag lay ... what? She put her hand into the dusty darkness and pulled the something out. It was a little, stiff-legged wooden doll, dressed in a long dark gown made of some rough material, and it wore a necklace of tiny seed pearls. Its head was tied up in a faded blue cotton bag.

The cart had come to a standstill, a little askew, near the gates of Mr Baldock's yard. He climbed down and opened the gates and the donkey trotted in.

Linda slipped her feet into her sandals, picked up the fallen drawer and flip-flopped up the hill.

'What's up?' asked Mr Baldock, as she approached.

She held up the small drawer.

'This fell off your cart.' The bag with the doll in it was hooked on her arm. She would have to tell him about it, of course, but she was reluctant to give him the curious little doll.

'Let's have a look,' Mr Baldock said, taking the drawer. He examined it carefully. 'Not a scratch, see. That's a bit of luck.'

'This fell out of it,' Linda said, holding up the bag.

He squinted at it. 'What is it?'

'An old workbag, I think. It ... it's got a doll in it.'

'Doll, eh?' Mr Baldock took the bag and looked inside.

'No use to me,' he said, handing it back to Linda. 'You have it, if you want it.'

Linda could hardly believe her luck. She went back to the doorstep, sat down, and took the doll out of the bag.

Her eager fingers pulled at the silken cord that fastened the blue cotton bag firmly round the doll's thin neck. The knots were many. Impatiently she worked at them, loosening them one by one. Why did the doll have her head in a bag, she wondered. Whoever had put the bag on had taken great care that it wouldn't fall off or be pulled off easily. Was it to keep the doll's face clean – or was its face so spoiled that the child who owned it did not want anyone to see it?

She was down to the last knot. She undid it, loosened the drawstring and slowly, carefully, pulled the bag off the doll's head.

A painted face stared up at her, the paint so bright and fresh it might have been put on that very morning. The tiny rosebud mouth was as red as blood, the eyes a deep cornflower blue under the delicate pencilled arches of the eyebrows. Its painted hair was black, with a straight, white centre-parting. Linda stared at it – and as she stared it seemed to her that the doll's expression changed. Yet how could it? It was only paint on wood, but the blue eyes had a new and glittering brilliance, the red mouth was set in a disapproving line, the dark brows had come together in a frown.

The afternoon was warm and airless, yet Linda felt a chill. She closed her eyes. When she opened them, the doll was just a wooden doll with a painted, expressionless face.

Linda laid the doll on the step. Black painted boots stuck stiffly up from under the hem of its long serge skirt, its arms lay straight at its sides, the painted face stared blankly at the sky and the neatly parted, painted hair shone like black satin in the sunlight. Yet Linda found herself glancing at it more than once, as she pulled the other things out of the bag.

Pieces of linen, velvet, satin, silk and fine lawn tumbled on to the step, together with lengths of ribbon and lace. There was a wool-worked needlecase, a small pair of scissors with a leather shield over the blades, a lacquered box holding a tape-measure, a pin-cushion, a brass thimble, a little red bonnet, and a red-and-white striped satin bag with a ribbon round the top, not much bigger than the bag that had covered the doll's head. There was also, surprisingly, a very small, very soft hairbrush.

Picking up what looked like a folded piece of dark red velvet, Linda discovered it was a doll's dress, with an embroidered yoke and the tiniest buttons she had ever seen sewn close together down the back. Searching more carefully among the other scraps, she found a tiny pair of black velvet mittens, a dark-blue cloak trimmed with white fur, a small, squashed, pale-blue velvet hat and another dress, made of gossamer-thin blue silk. They were all beautifully made. She put out her hand to pick up the doll, intending to take off its dull serge gown and dress it in its newly discovered finery.

Her fingers fumbled with the tiny hooks and

eyes at the front of the dress. She had thought it was black, but now that she held it in the light she saw that it was a very dark bottle-green. The hooks and eyes came undone at last. Linda raised the doll's arms and took hold of the hem of the skirt, preparing to pull the dress over the doll's head. She was immediately aware of resistance. She could not lift the skirt. It was as though invisible hands were holding it down, pushing her own hands away ... and the invisible hands were not the hands of a doll.

With a little cry of horror, Linda dropped the doll on to the step. It lay there with its arms upraised, motionless, expressionless, utterly wooden.

Trembling, Linda bundled everything back into the workbag, including the horrid little doll.

Then she heard her name being called. Startled, she looked up and saw Joanna Stone leaning out of an upper window in a house a little higher up the hill. Neither Angie nor Linda liked Joanna very much. She was too pushy, too bossy, too clever by half.

'What have you got there?' Joanna called.

'Just a bag,' said Linda, trying to hide it behind her on the step.

'Old Mr Baldock gave it to you, didn't he? *I* saw you. What's in it?'

'Nothing much.'

'Let's have a look ... wait a minute, I'll come down.'

That was the last thing Linda wanted, but there was no escape, unless she went inside and shut the door – which, of course, she couldn't very well do.

In a few moments, Joanna was standing before her, holding out her hand.

'Show me, then,' she demanded.

Reluctantly Linda handed her the workbag.

'Is this it?' asked Joanna, looking with disgust at the grubby old workbag, with its cross-stitch embroidery. 'What's in it?'

She pulled the wooden handles apart and peered into the bag. 'A doll!' she said, scornfully. 'Don't tell me you still play with dolls?'

'Not really,' Linda lied. 'I was only going to change...'

Joanna had thrust her hand into the bag and grasped the little wooden doll round its middle. She pulled it out into the sunlight, saying, 'It's hideous. I'm not surprised old Baldy gave it to you. I never saw such an ugly face.'

With the sickening click of a mousetrap, the upraised arms of the doll came down and snapped themselves tightly across the back of Joanna's hand.

Joanna dropped the workbag and screamed – but no sound came from her. Petrified, Linda sat staring at her. Her face was distorted with pain, her eyes wild and wide, her mouth held open in a silent scream.

Suddenly coming to life, Linda sprang to her feet and snatched at the doll, pulling at its arms, trying to prise them from Joanna's hand, not caring if she broke the beastly thing.

Under Linda's eager fingers the doll's arms rose smoothly and easily, leaving two deep red marks on the back of Joanna's hand.

'You might have warned me,' Joanna said, putting her hand to her mouth and sucking at it.

'I didn't know it was going to do that.' Linda stooped to pick up the workbag. 'I've only just had the thing.'

She looked at the doll she was holding. It was just an ordinary wooden doll, a little old-fashioned looking, perhaps, but pretty much like any other wooden doll; stiff legs, stiff arms, stiff body, egg-shaped head. It was difficult to believe there could possibly be anything odd about it.

Joanna was looking at it too, still sucking the back of her bruised hand.

'That's funny,' she said. 'Its face looks quite different now. It looked hideously cross before.'

'How could it?' Linda asked. There was a queer, tight feeling in her stomach. 'It's only a doll. Dolls can't change their expressions.'

But she knew this one could.

CHAPTER TWO

Tilda

'I'm boiling,' Joanna said. 'It's much too hot out here. I don't know how you can stand it.'

Joanna had a pale skin and shining, bright red hair. Linda was dark. The sun didn't bother her the way it bothered Joanna. All the same, it *was* very hot. The sun was shining straight down the little narrow street, the houses holding the heat in like the sides of an oven.

'Come indoors,' Joanna suggested. 'We'll get some ice cream from the fridge.'

This was an unheard-of generosity, not to be refused. Linda followed Joanna up the hill.

Five minutes later the girls were settled in Joanna's bedroom, each with a dish of vanilla ice-cream splashed with blackcurrant juice.

They scooped and scraped without speaking till the dishes were empty. Joanna put them on the window-sill and said, 'Now – let's see what else you've got in that bag.'

The bag was lying on the bed. Joanna took it

by its bottom corners and tipped it up.

'It's just bits of sewing stuff,' Linda said, 'and some clothes for the doll.'

Joanna had picked up the little hairbrush. Now she pounced on the red-and-white striped satin bag.

'What's this?'

'I don't know,' Linda said, uneasily. 'I haven't looked at that.'

'We'll look now,' said Joanna and pulled at the ribbon fastening the bag. 'It might be something valuable.'

She poked her fingers into the neck of the bag, gave a little shriek and dropped it on to the bed.

'What is it?' asked Linda, alarmed.

Joanna shook her head. 'Don't know – it feels – queer. Sort of hairy.'

Linda picked up the bag, tipped it upside-down and shook it.

A heap of something that looked like mouldy hay fell out.

Linda stared at it. Then she touched it gingerly with the tip of a nervous finger.

'It *is* hair!' she said, astonished.

'Ugh!' said Joanna, shuddering.

Linda picked up the bundle of hair and examined it more closely. Then she laughed. 'It's a *wig,*' she said, smoothing it over the top of her thumb. 'See – it's a wig for the doll! Made-out of somebody's hair. I wonder who made it?'

She turned the wig over. The hair had been most delicately and carefully stitched to a tiny bonnet-shaped piece of canvas.

'Put it on her,' Joanna said, snatching up the doll.

Linda felt again the sudden chill she had experienced outside in the sunny street, but Joanna had already taken the wig from her and was fitting it over the doll's black painted head.

'Give me the brush.'

'What?' said Linda.

'Give me the brush!' Joanna repeated. Her voice sounded strange. She was not looking at Linda but staring fixedly at the doll's face.

Linda handed her the little hairbrush. Slowly and rhythmically, Joanna began to brush the wig. Spiky and rough, the hair sprang up in all directions under the repeated strokes of the brush. It was wild and alive, crackling and flashing with electricity – and it was growing longer with every stroke.

Linda watched in fascinated horror as Joanna brushed the living hair, holding the doll firmly in her left hand. Her right arm moved faster and faster, the hair grew longer and longer. Then, under her left hand, Joanna felt a strange shivering, a trembling and quivering. The doll was growing too, swiftly and steadily, as the rough hair was smoothed.

'Stop!' cried Linda, terrified. 'Joanna, stop it!'

Joanna did not hear her. She was no longer holding the doll. It was standing by itself on the bed. Joanna's eyes were fixed on its face. That, too, had changed. It was a painted face no longer, but a real face, a living face, with glittering eyes, holding Joanna in its spell.

'Stop!' shrieked Linda again and darted forward, catching at Joanna's arm.

Joanna turned a dazed and bewildered face towards her and the brush dropped from her hand.

'What is it?' she whispered. 'What's happening?'

Linda could not answer her. She could not take her eyes from the doll that was not a doll. It had jumped off the bed and was standing before the little dressing-table mirror, brushing and brushing ... brushing and brushing. Now it was three feet tall ... taller ... taller ... nearly as tall as Linda herself. Still it brushed at its waist-length hair, but it grew no more. Linda could see its flushed and angry face reflected in the dressing-table mirror, not a doll's face, not exactly a child's face, yet it seemed to have become a child, of sorts.

With a cry of rage, the doll-child flung the hairbrush on to the floor and turned to face the two girls.

'*You* did this!' she stormed. 'Why? I am not myself! Who am I? What have you done to me?'

Her long fair hair floated about her, soft as silk, shining like moonlight, silvery pale. Yet her brows were dark and her glittering eyes seemed beetle-black and as hard as pebbles.

Then her fury left her. She shrugged her shoulders and smiled a mirthless smile as she fastened the front of the thick serge dress.

'We must make the best of it,' she said. 'You were not to know. How could you? What place is this?'

'It's – it's my bedroom,' Joanna faltered.

'What town – what town?' the doll-child asked, impatiently. 'What town – what country? Where am I?'

Half fearfully they told her, not knowing whether it would please her, but the smile came back and broadened into a grin of glee.

'Then all may not be lost,' she said. '*I am still here* . . .'

She lowered her voice and seemed to be speaking to herself rather than to the two girls. 'The question is – is *she* still here? How long have I been away, I wonder?' She touched the long string of pearls with her fingertips and asked, 'What year is this?'

They told her and she put her hands over her eyes and moaned.

'So long . . . so long . . . where is she now? Where is she now?'

'Who?' whispered Joanna.

'My other self,' said the doll-child. She touched the long pale hair with her fingertips. 'Where did this – this – wig – come from?'

'It was in that red-and-white bag,' Linda said, pointing towards the bed. She was still frightened, but she had stopped trembling. Joanna was holding her arm now, tightly, with both hands, as though their safety depended on keeping close to one another.

The doll-child turned towards the bed, and picked up the little red-and-white striped satin bag. A look of joy came into her face. She gave a laugh of triumph. 'So!' she said. 'Miss Lucy is still with us!'

'Lucy?' asked Linda, fearfully. 'Who's Lucy? I'm Linda – and this is my friend, Joanna.'

She would not have said 'my friend' a week ago, yesterday, nor this morning even, but at this moment, in the presence of this ... Thing ... she felt she needed a friend.

Linda might have felt unsure of herself but Joanna was beginning to recover some of her usual bounce.

'What's *your* name?' she asked.

'My name?' repeated the doll-child, as though the question surprised her. Then after a moment's hesitation, 'You may call me Tilda.'

'Tilda? What's that short for?' Joanna asked.

Ignoring Joanna's question the doll-child said, 'Now we will go for a walk. Fetch me a hat and a pair of gloves if you please.'

It was a command, not a request. Linda watched Joanna uneasily as she rummaged about in a drawer for the white silk gloves she had worn to her brother's wedding in the spring.

The hat was more of a problem. Apart from her school uniform beret and boater, the only hat Joanna possessed was an old brown woolly one, with a shaggy bobble on top.

'Most unsuitable,' said Tilda, impatiently.

'We don't wear hats much,' Joanna apologized. Then she remembered something.

She went into her older sister's room and came

back with a wide-brimmed straw sun-hat.

'That will be more becoming,' said the doll-child, trying it on. 'It's very plain, though. Is it quite fashionable, untrimmed?'

'Oh, yes,' said Joanna, eagerly. 'Some people stick brooches and things on them, but mostly they wear them like that.'

'Hmmm . . .' murmured the doll-child, standing before the mirror and arranging her long hair under the hat.

Behind her, on the bed, lay the tumble of odds and ends that had been in the workbag. She turned suddenly and pulled out a length of pale blue ribbon, which she wound round the crown of the hat, tying it in a bow at the back, leaving long ends trailing.

'That is a little more chic, I think,' she said, surveying her reflection. She turned to the watching girls. 'Now – when you are ready, we will go for our walk.'

She went to the door and opened it.

'I'm ready now,' Joanna said.

Tilda turned to look at her. 'You surely do not intend to go out in those garments?' she asked.

'Course.' Joanna looked down at her white T-shirt and blue cotton jeans. 'They're all right. They were clean on this morning.'

Linda was wearing shorts with her T-shirt. Her bare brown feet were thrust into a rather shabby pair of sandals which were unbuckled. Seeing the disapproving glance of the doll-child, she bent and fastened them.

'You do not wear socks or stockings?' There was a note of disbelief in Tilda's voice.

'*Stockings*?' said Linda. 'In this heat?'

Without a word, Tilda turned on her heel and marched across the landing – and Linda saw that under the long dark dress she was wearing little black boots with buttons up the sides and thick grey stockings.

'Doesn't she talk *funny*?' whispered Joanna, going towards the door.

From the top of the stairs Tilda called, sharply, 'It's not polite to whisper, Miss. Come along, now.'

The two girls exchanged glances. She sounded exactly like a school-mistress.

'You're not really going with her, are you?' Linda murmured.

'Of course,' said Joanna. 'She might get lost.'

'I hope she does,' Linda said, fiercely. 'You're mad to go with her.'

Nevertheless, as she followed Joanna down the stairs she knew that she, too, would be going on that walk. She had no choice. Some power, outside herself, compelled her to follow the curious little figure walking ahead of Joanna. A tight knot of fear twisted itself in Linda's stomach. What had they done? What mischief might they have caused by bringing the doll to life?

CHAPTER THREE

Angie

The walk was tedious. They had to keep stopping to let the doll-child rest. They had only gone as far as the top of the hill when Tilda said she must sit down and sank, exhausted, on to one of the iron seats by the castle wall.

'Don't you feel well?' Joanna asked, anxiously.

'I really do not know how I feel,' answered Tilda, faintly. 'I have certainly never felt like this before. I seem to have no strength in my limbs at all. It is as though I have had a long illness and am not yet quite recovered.'

'You poor thing,' said Joanna, sympathetically. 'Would you like to go back to the house?'

It was ridiculous the way Joanna was talking to her, Linda thought – as though she were a real person. Had she forgotten what had happened? She *mustn't* forget, nor must Linda. Tilda was a *doll* – a stiff little wooden doll with a painted face. How she had changed, what she had changed into, Linda did not know – but she certainly

31

wasn't a real child. She didn't even look like a real child, or talk like one. She looked, Linda decided, like somebody dressed up … yes, that was it … like a grown-up pretending to be a child.

'I shall be quite recovered in a moment,' she was saying, in her queer, precise way.

A few minutes later she stood up and they walked on towards the little town. They attracted many curious glances from passers-by. It was not surprising. Tilda looked very odd in her long dress and big straw hat, with her strange silvery hair flowing down over her shoulders to her waist.

'There seem to be a great many people about,' she said, as they approached the street where most of the shops were. A car whizzed by, close to the kerb and she gave a little shriek. 'And so many motor cars!'

'It's holiday time,' Joanna told her. 'The town's always full of visitors in the summer.'

'I dislike crowds,' said Tilda, so they turned off the High Street into a side road that led back to the harbour, stopping twice on the way for Tilda to catch her breath. When they reached the quayside they sat on a low stone wall. 'We'd better go home now,' said Linda, irritably.

She was tired of listening to this creature who talked like something out of a book, tired of listening to the sickening way Joanna spoke to her, tired of being stared at by strangers. There was nothing attractive about the doll-child. Her small, unsmiling face, with its thick dark brows and hard black eyes, was almost ugly.

Linda tried not to look into those hypnotic, glittering eyes. She had a feeling that if she did she would be as much under Tilda's spell as Joanna seemed to be.

'I do not wish to return to the house just yet,' Tilda said, rather sharply. 'I am not ill, simply a little tired.'

'I expect you're too hot in that thick dress,' Joanna said, soothingly. 'I should have lent you something thin to put on.'

'There she goes again,' thought Linda, 'talking to her as though she's real. It's horrible.'

'Yes,' said Tilda. 'Perhaps that would have been better. Or it might have been more sensible to wait until the cool of the evening to take our walk. It has been a long time since I last . . .' She broke off and stood up abruptly. 'I am rested now. Let us go to the Esplanade.'

'But that's miles . . .' Linda protested.

The Esplanade was a row of big Victorian houses on the cliff overlooking the harbour, not really so very far to walk but uphill all the way.

Linda could see them stopping every five minutes while Tilda clung to Joanna's arm, gasping for breath.

'You can see the Esplanade from here,' Joanna said, pointing. 'Why do you want to go there?'

'I have some unfinished business to attend to,' said the doll-child, with a grim little smile.

'Have you been there before, then?' asked Joanna, surprised.

'I'm going home,' Linda said. She had felt again that inexplicable chill, in spite of the warmth of the summer afternoon.

As she crossed the road towards the cobbled street where she lived, Linda heard Joanna say again, 'You've been here before? When?'

Of *course* she's been here before, thought Linda. It was obvious, wasn't it? The wooden doll in the workbag – and the wig. They were meant to go together, weren't they? But who had pulled the little blue bag over the doll's head and shut it away in that old chest of drawers ... and when? And why?

Angie was back. As she walked slowly up the steep, narrow street from the quay, Linda could see her standing on her front doorstep. She waved her arm vigorously but Angie was looking the other way.

Behind her, Linda could hear Joanna calling.

'Stop a minute, Linda. Wait for us.'

Linda turned. The other two were coming up behind her, Tilda leaning on Joanna's arm.

Linda stood still, waiting for them to catch up with her.

'We decided to wait till this evening to go to the Esplanade,' Joanna said, stopping beside her.

'You'll have to go on your own, then,' Linda told her. 'I promised to go swimming with Angie this evening.'

She turned to go on up the hill, but the doll-child put out her white-gloved hand and said, 'If you will be so kind as to give me your arm.'

Linda cringed. She did not want this ... creature ... to touch her. It had been bad enough handling her when she was just a wooden doll. All the same, she could hardly refuse ... She crooked her arm and Tilda slipped hers through it. The rough serge of her dress was hot and uncomfortable on Linda's bare skin, but she did not cling to Linda as she was clinging to Joanna.

Standing on the high stone step outside her front door, Angie watched the trio coming at a snail's pace up the narrow street. At first she thought Linda and Joanna were helping a little old lady to climb the hill, but as they drew nearer she realised her mistake. She stared with undisguised curiosity at the odd little figure walking between them.

'Hi, Angie!' Linda called, as soon as she was near enough to be heard. She waved her free arm.

'Hi!' Angie shouted. 'Hi, Jo!'

Joanna did not answer till they reached Angie's doorstep. Then she said, 'Hallo, Angie. This is Tilda. Tilda, this is Angie.'

'Hallo,' said Angie, with a grin, taking in every detail of the stranger's odd appearance.

'Good afternoon,' answered the doll-child, primly, adding, 'Angie ... your name is Angela, I presume?'

'That's right, Tilda,' said Angie, her grin broadening. 'And yours is Matilda, I presume.'

Linda suppressed a giggle. What a relief it was to have cheerful, cheeky Angie back, but how was she ever going to explain Tilda to her? She would never believe she was really a doll ...

The doll-child had let go of Linda's and Joanna's arms. She drew herself up and said, haughtily. 'In my case, Tilda is the diminutive of Clothilde.'

'That's French, isn't it?' asked Joanna, eagerly.

'We went to France for our summer holidays last year.'

'Are you French, then?' asked Angie, as though that explained everything.

Tilda inclined her head. 'I am of French origin,' she said. 'Now – if you will excuse me, I am rather fatigued. I should like to lie down for an hour. Come, Joanna.'

With a stiff little bow to Linda and Angie she took Joanna's arm and they turned to go on up the hill.

'See you,' Joanna called, over her shoulder.

'I am of French origin,' mimicked Angie, watching Joanna help Tilda up the steps to her house. 'Why didn't she say she had a French grandmother, or mother, or father, or whatever? Where on earth did you find her? She's weird.'

'I found her in an old workbag,' thought Linda, but it was hardly the answer Angie would be expecting.

'Is she a visitor,' Angie asked.

'I think so,' Linda said. She meant she hoped so. She hoped the doll-child would disappear as swiftly and strangely as she had appeared.

'Where's she staying?' Several of the houses in the street had Bed and Breakfast notices in their windows.

Until that moment it had not occurred to Linda to ask herself that question. Where *was* the doll-child to stay? She could hardly stay with Linda or Joanna – how could she be explained to their parents? Yet, presumably, she must sleep somewhere. It was a nightmare, that's what it was – a bad dream. No one was going to believe that she and Joanna had created Tilda ... She wasn't even sure she believed it herself.

'I don't know where she's staying,' she said, with perfect truth.

'How long's she here for?'

'I don't know that, either,' Linda said, miserably.

'Well, she needn't bother us much,' Angie said, grinning. 'She seems to have taken up with Joanna. But, French or not, you've got to admit she's weird. Those clothes! And that hair! It looks like a wig.'

'It is,' Linda said – and then wished she hadn't.

'No! Is it? You're joking!'

Was this the time to tell Angie the truth? Linda looked up and down the familiar, sane, sun-shafted street and said, 'Angie, listen. I've got something to tell you ...'

'And I've got something to tell you,' Angie said. 'Gran's coming to stay with us while Nan and

Grandad have a holiday.' Gran was Angie's great-grandmother. She was over eighty, but lively and active still. The only trouble was that she was very fussy. She had once been in service in one of the grand houses in the Esplanade and she liked everything done 'just right'.

'When's she coming?' Linda asked. If Gran was going to stay in Angie's house, she would have Angie's room, which meant . . .

'Dad's going to fetch her this evening,' Angie said. 'So I'll be staying with you tonight. What were you going to tell me?'

'It doesn't matter,' Linda said. 'I'll tell you later. You probably won't believe it, anyway.'

Linda was right, of course. Angie didn't believe her. Well – who would? The two girls had tea in Linda's house while Angie's mother made Angie's room ready for Gran. After the meal, Linda took Angie up to her bedroom where she found the spare bed already made up.

'Why didn't Mum tell me?' Linda wanted to know. 'Why didn't you?'

'In case Gran wouldn't come,' said Angie. 'You know what she's like. Now, what's this mysterious something you want to tell me about?'

Linda told her.

'You must think I'm potty,' said Angie, laughing. 'Or else *you* are. You've been out in the sun too long.' This was one of Gran's favourite sayings – anyone who behaved in the least oddly had been out in the sun too long.

'I knew you wouldn't believe me,' Linda said.

Angie snorted. 'Well, of course I don't believe you. I never heard anything so daft.'

They were sitting on the windowsill. The sun had shifted and the street was full of shadows and odd little patches of light. Joanna came out of her front door carrying something in her hand. Linda knew at once what it was. She opened the window and called, 'We're upstairs, Jo. Come on up.'

'Can't stop,' Joanna called. 'Tilda wants me to take her up to the Esplanade. I've brought back that old bag Mr Baldock gave you. I'll put it inside your front door.'

'Jo!' shouted Linda. 'I want you to tell Angie about the doll.'

'Doll?' said Joanna. 'What doll? I don't know anything about a doll ...'

Linda and Angie did not go swimming. They stayed up in Linda's room, hardly speaking to one another.

'I'm not going anywhere with you, Linda

40

Barnes, till you admit you've been talking a load of rubbish,' Angie had declared, after Joanna's astonishing denial.

Linda wouldn't admit it – how could she? She knew that what she had said was true. The doll's clothes, the little hairbrush, the blue cotton bag, the red-and-white striped satin bag, didn't convince Angie. When Linda found a few straw-coloured hairs inside it, she said, 'So? Somebody put some hair in a bag. It's probably what they called a "hair tidy".'

'I'm telling you the *truth*,' Linda insisted. Angie's chin set in a stubborn line. She took one of Linda's books from the shelf and sat on the windowsill to read it.

The two girls seldom fell out over anything, but Linda knew that if she persisted with the tale of the afternoon's magical happenings, there would be a terrible quarrel. So she pottered about, doing this and that, saying nothing while Angie read her way steadily through a book she had read before.

At about seven o'clock Angie's father arrived with Gran. He parked his car at the top of the hill and helped the old lady down to the house. Angie's mother ran out and tried to take Gran's other arm.

'Don't fuss! Don't fuss!' said the old lady. 'I don't need two of you to help me. I've still got the use of my legs.'

'Just listen to her!' Angie said, laughing and leaning out of the window. 'Hallo, Gran!' she shouted.

Linda went to the window and looked out. The old lady waved at her. 'Hallo, young Linda,' she called, smiling up at her.

Out of the corner of her eye, Linda saw Joanna and Tilda coming up the hill. Tilda was wearing Joanna's best blue silk dress. It was made in an old-fashioned style, with lace at the neck and wrists. She wore long white socks and the black patent leather shoes Joanna had had for her brother's wedding. The straw hat did not look at all out of place with this outfit. Linda leaned out of the window to get a better look.

'Here comes Joanna,' she said.

Gran had reached Angie's doorstep. She turned to see where Linda was looking.

Then she staggered and collapsed on to the doorstep.

'Miss Lucy!' they heard her say. 'Oh, my dear soul! Miss Lucy!'

CHAPTER FOUR

Gran

Angie raced out of the room and down the stairs the moment she saw her great-grandmother stagger and appear to fall. Linda went after her, her mind in a turmoil.

'Miss Lucy,' Gran had said. Linda had heard her distinctly. It was the sight of the doll-child coming up the hill that made Gran stumble, Linda was certain.

Angie's mother was helping Gran into the house when the girls reached the street, scolding her much as she might have scolded Angie or Linda for doing something silly.

'You should have taken my arm, like I wanted. You're too independent for your own good. You could have hurt yourself, going down like that, on that hard step. Come into the front room now and I'll get you a nice cup of tea.'

Angie's father came up behind the two girls, a little out of breath. He had been on his way back to the car to fetch Gran's things when he heard his wife call out as Gran staggered on to the door-step.

'Is she all right?' he asked, anxiously.

'Of course I'm all right!' shrilled Gran. 'Don't make such a fuss! Can't I sit down for a minute if I want to?'

'She's all right,' grinned Angie. 'If Gran's cross, she's all right.'

All the same, she went into the house to make sure.

Linda stood on the step, watching Joanna and Tilda creeping towards her. 'So Miss Lucy is still with us,' the doll-child had said. What did it all mean? Why had Gran been so startled at the sight of her?

Tilda was walking with head bent, taking no notice of her surroundings. Joanna was watching Angie's father getting Gran's luggage out of the car.

She stopped when she reached Linda. 'Has Angie got a visitor?' she asked, with a superior smirk. Although Joanna's house was bigger than Linda's or Angie's, her parents never took summer visitors.

'Only Gran,' Linda said.

'Her great-grandmother,' Joanna explained to Tilda.

'A great-grandmother?' said Tilda. 'She must be very old.'

'Ancient,' Joanna told her. 'She lived here during the First World War.'

'Ah . . .' breathed Tilda, glancing up at Angie's house. Gran was standing in the front room window, peering out at the girls.

The doll-child looked at Linda. 'The old have strange fancies,' she said. 'It is not always wise to listen to them.'

It sounded like a warning – and now Linda found herself looking, against her will, at that strange, unfriendly face. Fleetingly the hard black eyes looked straight into hers and she felt chilled.

Then, behind her, Angie's cheerful voice called from the passageway, 'Hallo, Jo. Hallo, Tilly. Enjoy your walk?'

Angie's habit of shortening or changing people's names had often caused annoyance but never before had it produced such an angry reaction as it did now. The doll-child turned a fiercely distorted face towards her. Her black eyes blazed, her mouth was twisted with fury as she spat out, 'Address me by my proper name, Miss, or it will be the worse for you.'

'Okay . . . okay . . .' said Angie, unruffled. 'Keep your hair on.'

At this, the doll-child let out a little scream and put her hand up instinctively to touch the shining tresses that fell about her shoulders.

'Did you get up to the Esplanade, Jo?' Linda asked, hastily.

Joanna nodded. 'Yes. Tilda wanted to call at one of the houses where she stayed when she was here before, but there wasn't anyone at home.'

The doll-child glared venomously at Angie, then at Linda.

'Come now, Joanna,' she ordered, turning and dragging Joanna with her. 'We must go. I am very tired.'

'Sorry,' said Joanna, meekly and walked obediently on up the hill.

'Well!' said Angie, watching them. 'I never thought I'd see Joanna Stone being bossed about like that. She seems to be right under that weirdo's thumb.'

'Under her spell, you mean,' murmured Linda but Angie ignored her.

'I think you're right about the hair,' she said. 'It *is* a wig.' She laughed. 'Did you see the way she grabbed at it when I told her to keep her hair on?'

'I *know* it's a wig. I told you it was. Joanna put it on her ... Oh, Angie, you must believe me,'

Linda said, desperately. 'Can't you *see* there's something odd about her? She's not *real*. A real child wouldn't be wandering about in a strange town on her own, with nowhere to stay . . .'

'You're not still on about that, are you?' Angie said, crossly. 'You heard what Jo said. They called at a house on the Esplanade, where she stayed before. She was obviously supposed to stay there this time. After all, she's old enough to be allowed to travel on her own.'

'Without any luggage?' said Linda, scathingly. 'Without even a toothbrush?'

'Oh, shut up!' cried Angie and stamped back into the house.

Linda sat down on the step and put her head in her hands. She heard Angie say, with a note of triumph in her voice, 'She left her luggage at the station, stupid. You can see she's not very strong. She couldn't possibly lug a suitcase all the way to the Esplanade.'

Thoughts and images whirled about in Linda's confused mind. She saw a wooden doll, with a prim, painted face – a wooden doll with a fierce, angry expression – a wooden doll snapping its stiff arms down on Joanna's hand ... Yet Joanna seemed to have forgotten about the doll, which meant she had forgotten the wig and the hairbrush – and the way the straw-like hair had begun to shine and grow, as the doll became a child and the child grew and grew...

With a shudder of remembered horror, Linda stood up. Angie was right. It was a ridiculous story. Nobody could possibly believe it. Did she really believe it herself? Had she, perhaps, fallen asleep on the step that afternoon and dreamed the whole thing ... was Tilda just a rather odd little girl who had been sent to the seaside for a holiday? But where was she staying? Not on the Esplanade – whoever heard of a guest house with no one at home to open the door to the guests?

Her thoughts were interrupted by the sound of a door being shut, higher up the hill. Joanna came out of her house and walked slowly down to her.

'She's asleep,' she said, in answer to Linda's unspoken question. 'I've put her in the spare room.'

'What did Mrs Porter say?' asked Linda.

Joanna's parents had gone away for the weekend. Their neighbour was 'keeping an eye on things' and seeing to meals for Joanna and her sister.

'I let her think Mum had forgotten to tell her Tilda was coming,' Joanna said. 'And Sam doesn't care. You know what she's like.'

Samantha was nearly seventeen and far too engrossed in her own affairs to pay much attention to her young sister.

She came out of the house now and slammed the door shut behind her. She was wearing pink jeans and a glitzy blue sleeveless top. Her long dark hair was wound round her head and threaded through with loops of pearls.

'Sam! Where did you get those pearls?' cried Joanna, moving quickly towards her.

'Out of your room, little sister,' said Samantha, tossing her head.

'Put them back! They're Tilda's.'

'*They're Tilda's*!' mocked Samantha. 'Well, Tilda's asleep. She doesn't wear her beads in bed. Anyway, she borrowed my hat without asking. See you tomorrow. Don't wait up. Disco doesn't finish till twelve.'

With a wave of her many-braceleted arm she went on up the hill.

'Sam ... come back!' Joanna shouted, but Samantha ignored her.

'Tilda will be *furious*,' Joanna said. 'She was cross enough when she found I'd given you that old workbag.'

'But it's mine,' Linda protested. 'Mr Baldock gave it to me, you know he did.'

'She says it's hers,' Joanna said. 'She says it's always been hers. She wants it back.'

'Well, she can't have it,' Linda said, stubbornly.

'Oh, come on, Linda,' Joanna coaxed. 'It's only a rubbishy old bag.'

'Why does *she* want it, then?'

Joanna hesitated then said, 'I don't know. She just said she must have it back.'

Linda hadn't really wanted the workbag, but now it seemed important to keep it, at least till she had been through it to see what could be so important to the doll-child. Maybe there was some way of changing her back into a doll . . .

Then came the sound of someone tapping on a windowpane. Linda looked up and saw Gran beckoning her.

'I'll think about it,' she said and ran into the house.

Gran turned away from the window the moment Linda moved. If she had not, she would have seen Joanna go quickly up the neighbouring steps to the open front door of Linda's house.

'My, how you've grown!' Gran said, when Linda appeared in the doorway. Linda smiled. Gran always said that, when she hadn't seen her for some time.

Gran was alone in the room, sitting on a high-backed chair by the window, with a cup of tea and a plate of biscuits on a little table nearby.

'Have a biscuit,' she said, pushing at the plate.

Linda didn't really want a biscuit, but she took one and began to nibble it round the edges.

'Where's Joanna's friend?' Gran asked.

'Asleep,' said Linda. 'She gets tired easily.'

'A-a-ah,' said Gran. 'She does, does she?'

They looked at one another. There was a heavy silence in the room. 'She *knows*,' thought Linda.

Gran gave a funny little laugh. 'I'm just a silly old woman,' she said. 'Fancy thinking that child was Miss Lucy! But she did look like her, from a distance. Oh, my word, she did! It was the hair, I think. Miss Lucy had such lovely hair ... and she had a dress just that colour blue ... It gave me quite a turn, I can tell you, seeing her coming up the hill like that. Many's the time I've watched Miss Lucy coming up this very street to meet me. I had charge of her, on Nanny's afternoon off, you know. I used to let her stay down by the quay while I came up here to see my mother. She loved watching the boats. It was a lot busier down there in those days than it is now. "When the harbour clock strikes half past three," I used to say, "you come and fetch me." She was a good girl, Miss

51

Lucy. I knew she wouldn't go wandering off...'

Gran's voice trailed off and she stared out of the window, down towards the quayside. The shadows had lengthened, filling the quiet street. Here and there, on the houses opposite, a high window glinted, a patch of roof-top glowed, where the sun slanted between the chimneypots or down a narrow alleyway.

'We had some good times,' Gran said. 'I was hardly more than a child myself. Just thirteen, I was, when I first went up to the house on the Esplanade – and Miss Lucy barely six.' She sighed. 'It was all a long time ago – a long time ago.'

There was a sound in the hall. Angie's mother bustled in, followed by Angie.

'Finished your tea, Gran?' she asked, taking the cup and plate. 'Better not have any more – you'll spoil your supper. Eight o'clock suit you? I know you like to go to bed early.'

'No, I don't,' Gran said, tartly. 'But everybody seems to think I should.'

'Don't be silly, now, Gran,' said Angie's mother. As she went out she said to Linda, 'Don't let her get started on one of her tales, now, or you'll be here all night. She and her Miss Lucy. The tales she's got to tell! Miss Lucy's an old lady

52

now, but Gran still thinks of her as a little girl.'

'She was just a little girl when I knew her,' Gran said. 'Poor little soul.'

'What happened to her?' whispered Linda, hardly daring to ask.

Gran looked at her sadly. 'Don't you know, my dear?' she asked. 'The poor child was bewitched.'

PART TWO

The House
on the Esplanade:
1919–1920

CHAPTER FIVE

Miss Lucy

Six-year-old Lucy Tregoran knelt on the nursery window-seat watching the boats in the bay. The March wind blew a flurry of rain against the window, blurring her view. She sighed, but she stayed where she was. She spent hours staring out of that window, a prisoner of the weather and the whims of Nanny.

Nanny was asleep in the old rocking chair by the fire. She was old now and a bit rheumaticky. No more walks for her on frosty winter mornings, nor on blustery March afternoons. She had looked after Lucy's father and his four older sisters when they were children and she had not been young, even then. Now she stayed indoors – unless the sun was shining and the air was warm – which meant Lucy had to stay in, too.

The big house on the Esplanade was a gloomy place for a lonely only child. No sounds of music, no laughter, no cheerful chatter ever drifted up from the downstairs rooms to the nursery now.

Some of the many rooms had been shut up, the curtains partly drawn, the furniture shrouded in dust sheets. Sometimes Lucy would turn a door-knob and peep into one of the dim rooms on the floor below and try to remember who had slept in the big cold bed before her father went away. She could never remember. She was barely three years old when her father went off to war. That was when the changes began. The gardener's boy had gone first and then Jack, the boy who came to clean the knives and polish the boots and carry in the coals. Too young to join the Army, he had stowed away on a ship bound for foreign parts – only it hadn't been. It had only gone as far as Liverpool. Within three months Jack was back home, but he never returned to the house on the Esplanade.

By the time Jack was back with his family, Lucy's father had been killed in France. Money was short now. Economies had to be made. There was a nursery maid in those days, a bright, cheer-ful girl who came at once if Lucy cried in the night, nursed her when she was unwell, read to her, sung to her, played with her, taught her her letters and her numbers. She it was who taught Lucy to dress herself, do up her buttons, fasten her shoes and save Nanny's stiff fingers from trouble and pain – but as soon as Lucy was able to do these things for herself, poor Gwennie had to go.

The parlourmaid was next and then the house-maid. Runaway Jack's sister, Bessie, came as a kitchenmaid but ended up as the maid-of-all-work; housemaid in the mornings, parlourmaid in the afternoons and kitchenmaid whenever Cook needed her. That was when the sun was shut out, the pictures turned face to the wall and the furniture covered up in all the unused rooms. It would have been too much for Bessie to manage on her own.

Lucy saw very little of her mother. The child lived up in the nursery with Nanny, watching what she could see of the world from the window-seat. Bessie came up every morning to light the fire and looked in three or four times a day in case Nanny had forgotten to tend it.

Although Nanny seldom left the house, she insisted on taking her afternoon off every week. Lucy would be sent down to the kitchen in the basement where Cook would let her help with making a cake or a pie, or, even better, would show her how to make toffee or coconut ice.

Cook had been in the house a long time – long before Lucy's mother and father were married.

Lucy loved hearing her tell tales of the old days, when the house had been full of people and Cook had had what she called 'proper cooking' to do.

On her last visit to the kitchen, Lucy had learned that orders had been given for the unused rooms to be opened up again and since it would be so much extra for Bessie, a new maid-of-all-work was coming.

'My sister Elsie,' Bessie said, proudly. 'Your Ma asked me if I knew of a strong and willing girl. I told her. "Elsie," I said. "She's thirteen now and a good little worker, even though I says it myself." So I'm fetching her up on my afternoon off, to see if she'll suit.'

Today was Bessie's afternoon off. Lucy had seen her soon after twelve o'clock, hurrying, head bent against the wind, down the long slope of the Esplanade. She could see the end of the street where Bessie lived, on the far side of the harbour, but she hadn't been able to pick her out among all the other people moving to and fro along the quayside.

She pressed her nose to the cold glass. It was nearly three o'clock. Surely they must come soon? Then she saw them, two girls clinging to one another, bent under a big umbrella, their long skirts flapping in the wind.

A little squiggle of excitement ran through Lucy. If Elsie was anything like big, cheerful Bessie, it would be very nice having her in the house.

It was a fortnight since cheeky, chatty Elsie had come to the house on the Esplanade. Already great changes had taken place, the greatest being that Lucy was to go out more.

'That child looks real peaky,' Elsie had said, on her second day. 'If you ask me, M'm, she's not getting enough fresh air. A good brisk walk is what she needs. Put some colour in her cheeks.'

Bessie had been horrified to hear her sister talk like this to her new mistress, but Mrs Tregoran had said, 'She does look a little pale. I think you're right. She's been shut up in this stuffy old house far too long. We all have. Fresh air is what we all need, to blow the cobwebs away.'

So the curtains were taken down to be cleaned, the windows opened, the dust sheets gathered up and the unused rooms swept and dusted – and every day Lucy went out for half an hour with Elsie. Sometimes, on fine days, she was allowed to go down into the garden by herself, on condition she did nothing to annoy the crotchety old gardener.

'She don't need Nanny watching her all the time, not when she's in her own garden,' Elsie had said – and Lucy's mother had looked at Lucy and replied, as though she had only just realized it, 'Of course she doesn't. She's not a baby.'

So Nanny was left to doze and dream in the nursery and came downstairs only when she felt she could – life for Lucy began to be fun.

People came to the house now. There were little tea-parties and supper-parties and men's loud voices and laughter in the hall. Lucy's mother stopped wearing dismal black clothes and began to look pretty again. She even noticed that some of Lucy's things were too tight, or short, or shabby and took her into town to buy new ones.

That summer was the happiest Lucy had ever known. Unless it was raining, Elsie had charge of her now, on Nanny's afternoons off. They went for long walks, they wandered round the town, explored the old castle, visited the park and the museum or the beach. Sometimes Elsie would leave Lucy down by the quay while she ran home to see her mother for half an hour. At half past three Lucy would walk up the steep, narrow street and be taken into Elsie's crowded little house for a mug of milk and a biscuit or a piece of cake. Elsie had younger brothers and sisters as well as older ones. Often the little kichen seemed to be full of children, other people's as well as the ones who lived there. Lucy never realized that they had come in specially, to see the 'little girl from the big house', with her beautiful long golden hair and her nice, new clothes.

'Not a word to Nanny, now,' Elsie would warn, as she and Lucy walked home. 'Nor to your Ma. We don't want 'em putting a stop to our little outings, do we?'

Certainly, Lucy did not want anyone to put a stop to anything. She had never enjoyed herself so much.

One wet afternoon when Lucy was in the kitchen rolling out a piece of left-over pastry, Bessie came in saying, 'Dr Marchbanks is here again. That's the third time this week.'

'Must be serious,' Elsie said, grinning.

'Is Mama not well?' Lucy asked, alarmed.

'As well as can be expected,' said Elsie, cheerfully. 'Touch of spring fever, if you ask me. That's when it started, anyway.'

'That tongue of yours will get you into trouble one day, my girl,' said Cook, glaring at her.

The weather cleared up later that afternoon and, while they were out for their walk, Elsie asked casually, 'How would you fancy having a new Pa, Miss Lucy?'

Such an idea had never occurred to Lucy. She could not imagine what life would be like with a papa. She could hardly remember her father, though she knew what he looked like, of course, from the photograph in Mama's bedroom.

'I don't know,' she said, thoughtfully. 'Why? Am I going to have one?'

'Could be,' Elsie said. 'Only don't say I told you.'

Lucy was mystified. 'Who will it be?' she wanted to know.

'Wait and see,' said Elsie.

A few days later Bessie came up to the nursery and spoke to Nanny and Nanny began bustling about, making Lucy change into one of her new dresses, washing her face and hands, re-doing her hair, brushing it till it shone like gold.

'You're to go down to the drawing-room at four o'clock,' she said.

It was a long time since Lucy had been told to go down to the drawing-room. She felt a little apprehensive as she went slowly down the stairs behind Nanny.

'Miss Lucy, Ma'am,' said Nanny, at the drawing-room door.

'Thank you, Nanny,' said Mrs Tregoran and Nanny went away, leaving Lucy standing nervously just inside the drawing-room. Her mother was not alone. There was a stranger standing with his back to the fireplace, a big man, with thick black curly hair, a black beard and moustache, black eyebrows and deep-set eyes, so dark they looked like shiny bits of coal. 'Lucy,' said Mrs Tregoran, 'this is Dr Marchbanks. We are to be married next month. He will be your new papa, so come and say "How do you do?" to him.'

'How do you do?' whispered Lucy, looking up at the fearsome stranger.

'How do you do, Lucy,' Dr Marchbanks answered in a deep, husky voice. 'Are you a good child?'

Lucy didn't quite know how to answer this. She thought she was good, but you could never tell with grown-ups. Nanny sometimes scolded her for doing things she didn't even know she wasn't supposed to do. . . .

'I think so,' she said, hoping her mother would come to her rescue.

'She is a little shy,' said Mrs Tregoran. 'She is

not used to meeting strangers.'

Dr Marchbanks smiled. Lucy saw his teeth gleam white for an instant above the bushy black beard.

'We shall soon change that,' he said.

Then he began to ask Lucy questions – what did she do all day, up in the nursery? Could she read ... write ... do her sums?

'I am afraid she has not had much schooling,' sighed her mother. 'I should have seen to it myself, I suppose. But there are plenty of books in the nursery – all her father's old schoolbooks and most of the books he and his sisters had as children ... plenty to keep her occupied. She reads quite well, I believe.'

It was true. Lucy did read quite well. She had nothing much else to do – and when Nanny was not dozing by the fire she was quite happy to put her spectacles on and help Lucy with whatever book she had chosen to read – story books, history books, geography books, even science books, one was as good as another to her.

'Schooling is not quite so important for a girl as for a boy,' said Dr Marchbanks, 'but the child must not be allowed to grow up totally uneducated. We must see what we can do to improve matters.'

A few minutes later, Lucy was back in the nursery.

'Well,' said Nanny, changing Lucy out of her new clothes, 'What did you think of Dr Marchbanks?'

Lucy could hardly say that she did not like him at all, so she said, 'I think he wants me to be educated.'

'More than likely,' Nanny said, tidying Lucy's hair. 'There'll be some changes, you mark my words. Things will be very different when he's master here.'

How different no one could ever have guessed.

Lucy's mother married Dr Marchbanks at the beginning of September. They spent the rest of the month in France, returning to the house on the Esplanade in the first week of October.

From the moment of their return, things began to change. Fires were lit in all the downstairs rooms every day, instead of just in the one where Lucy's mother was. Cook had more and better meals to prepare, which pleased her. The doctor was a big man. He liked his food and ate heartily. In the second week of October, Phipps, the parlourmaid, came back. (Lucy never quite understood why Elsie was Elsie and Bessie was Bessie but Phipps was Phipps, though everyone knew her first name was Mabel.) Bessie went back to being housemaid, which pleased her because she had always said she was too big (and too clumsy) to be a proper parlourmaid.

Lucy had to be dressed in her best and taken down to the drawing-room every afternoon when her mother and the doctor were at home. Old Nanny mumbled and grumbled at having to go up and down so many stairs. Dr Marchbanks, standing in front of the fireplace (blocking off the fire with his great bulk) would ask Lucy questions about her day. What had she learned? Had she been for a walk, had any exercise? Where had she been? So – she had spent the afternoon reading and drawing, had she? What had Nanny been doing while Lucy was occupying herself?

Then, one foggy November afternoon, Phipps, carrying the tea-tray, found Lucy standing outside the drawing-room door, alone, tapping so timidly she could not possibly have been heard.

'Knock hard, Miss Lucy,' Phipps said. 'Then count three and open the door. Let me go in first.'

Lucy did as she was told, opening the door such a little way that Phipps had to push it with her elbow before she could take the tray through.

'Miss Lucy, ma'am,' she announced. 'Nanny is indisposed.'

'Oh, dear!' said the new Mrs Marchbanks. 'Nothing serious, I hope?'

'It's the damp, ma'am,' Phipps said. 'It gets into her bones.'

'Poor Nanny,' murmured Lucy's mother, sympathetically, 'Poor old thing.'

'It's high time she was pensioned off,' Dr Marchbanks said, firmly.

'But she's been with us such a long time...' began Lucy's mother.

'All the more reason for letting her go,' said Dr Marchbanks. 'What has the child been doing today? Mooning about up there in the nursery, I'll be bound. She should have a governess. She *must* have a governess, if she is not to grow up entirely uneducated. As I told you, my dear, I heard of an excellent woman while we were in France. Clothilde Dupont. Her grandfather was a Frenchman, I believe. She has spent a great deal of time in France, so if Lucy learns nothing else, she will at least have excellent French. Which is more than can be said for you, my dear,' he added, with an unkind little laugh. 'I have her address. You shall write to her today.'

*

It was the last day of December. Nanny had been given a month's notice that dark November day and had gone from the house the week before Christmas, weeping and protesting that Mr Robert (Lucy's father) had promised his mother he would look after her all her days.

'Mr Robert is no longer with us,' Dr March-banks had said, 'and I made no such promise to anyone. Neither did my wife.'

No one said anything to Lucy about Nanny's departure, but Elsie moved out of the attic room she shared with Bessie and came to sleep in Nanny's room, which opened on to the night nursery.

'Can't leave the poor little mite on her own,' Elsie said. 'If the doctor don't like it, he can lump it.'

No one expected Lucy to do any lessons just before Christmas, nor just after. She was so happy and excited at seeing the great house decorated with greenery, and sharing in all the preparations going on down in the kitchen, that she quite forgot her new governess was supposed to arrive at the end of the month.

Then the year was almost over, the Christmas food had all been eaten, the holly berries had shrivelled, the Christmas tree in the hall was dropping needles on the carpet, making Bessie grumble, as she went to sweep up for the second time that day. She was on her hands and knees with a dustpan and brush when there was a loud, sharp knocking on the front door. Then the bell was jangled, impatiently.

Bessie scrambled to her feet to get out of sight before Phipps came to open the front door.

Lucy, who had been sitting on the bottom step of the stairs watching Bessie, stayed where she was. Passing her, Phipps said, 'You'd better move, Miss Lucy. You don't know who it might be. You don't want your new Pa to see you there.'

She opened the front door as the bell rang again. Lucy, going slowly and reluctantly up the stairs, looked back over her shoulder.

On the doorstep stood a tall, thin woman dressed in black. Beside her on the step was a black leather hold-all. In her gloved hands she held a large black handbag, an umbrella and an embroidered canvas workbag, with wooden handles.

'My name is Dupont,' she said, in a crisp, commanding voice. 'I am expected. Tell your mistress that I am here.'

Then she raised her head and looked at Lucy, who had paused, halfway up the stairs. She did not smile. She did not speak, but her hard bright eyes filled Lucy with an inexplicable feeling of fear. She turned and ran up the stairs to the silent and empty nursery.

CHAPTER SIX

The Governess

'I don't like her,' Cook said, fiercely beating eggs in a basin. 'There's something not quite right about her. You mark my words, there'll be trouble, sure as eggs is eggs.'

'She's got funny eyes,' Elsie said. 'It's like she's looking right through you and out the other side.'

'And bringing her own furniture! The cheek of it! Ours isn't good enough, I s'pose. Well, she needn't expect me to polish her precious chest of drawers. It's bad enough having it stuck up there on the landing like that. I scraped my shin on it this morning.'

Bessie stuck out a plump leg and rubbed it gingerly.

The carrier's cart had come slowly up the long hill from the town the day after Miss Dupont's arrival, bringing, not a tin trunk as might have been expected, but two trunk-sized parcels, wrapped in sacking and oilskin and securely bound with thick rope. The 'parcels' had to be taken in through the front door and up the wide main staircase because they were too heavy and cumbersome to be carried down the basement steps and up again by way of the narrow back stairs.

'Ah! My beautiful furniture!' cried the governess, when she was told the carrier had brought something for her. She stood at the top of each flight of stairs, watching as Bessie and Elsie and the carrier struggled up with their heavy burdens, calling out to them every now and then to take care.

When the ropes were undone and the 'parcels' unwrapped, the 'beautiful furniture' turned out to be a travelling chest of drawers in two parts, like the ones sometimes used by Army officers. The bottom half had two long, deep drawers and the top half one long drawer and three small ones in a row above it.

As there was no space in the governess's room, unless some of the existing furniture was moved out, the chest had to stand on the landing, near the top of the back staircase. It was a very inconvenient place to put it, since it jutted out a little across the top step, but there was nowhere else it could stand without blocking a doorway.

The governess watched anxiously as Bessie and

the carrier lifted the top half into place, crying, 'Take care! Do not scratch it. Take care! Do not tip, I beg you. Do not tip!'

Afterwards the carrier sat down in the kitchen and had three cups of tea and one of Cook's pasties and said he reckoned he'd earned it.

'She gave him sixpence,' Bessie grumbled, when he had gone, 'but not a word of thanks to Elsie and me. Not a word. "You may go now," she said, like she was the mistress. "I will unlock the drawers presently and see that everything is as it should be."'

'She didn't want us to see what was in it,' Elsie said.

'Huh!' snorted Bessie. 'What's she got that's so special?'

'She's a queer one and no mistake,' Cook said, pouring Bessie another cup of tea. 'I only hope Miss Lucy won't suffer because of it.'

Lucy, like Cook, disliked the new governess. Gone were the old, easy days of doing lessons when she felt like it or when Nanny was prepared to help her. The old schoolroom, which had been a lumber room for years, had been cleared out and cleaned and now Lucy spent long hours there every day, except Sundays, working at the lessons

Miss Dupont set for her. Sometimes the governess sat beside her to explain something and Lucy would feel a strange chill at her nearness. There was no warmth in her. Her hands were always icy cold, her voice was harsh. She seldom smiled and when she did the smile was not reflected in her eyes. Most of the time, though, she sat at her own desk, facing Lucy. Her pale oval face was expressionless, her black hair, with its perfect centre-parting, shone like satin and her hard eyes were always fixed upon the child.

Sometimes Lucy felt compelled to look up and meet that penetrating gaze. Then it would seem to her that a shiver ran through her, the room blurred and there was a strange whispering in her ears. Whatever work she was doing she did with a speed and accuracy that would have astonished her mother – or anyone else who saw her. Afterwards, Lucy would feel utterly exhausted, limp as an old rag lying rotting in the sun – but the pages of her exercise books would be covered with neat writing or correctly worked out sums. There were times when it seemed that she sat at her desk for days on end, under the spell of those hard bright eyes. Long after her lessons were ended she would sit in the schoolroom in a daze, quite unaware that the governess had gone.

'That child's being made to work too hard,' Bessie said, coming down with Lucy's tea-tray one miserable January afternoon. 'She hardly knows whether she's coming or going half the time. When I took her tea up she was still at her desk. She asked me if she'd had her lunch! Couldn't remember what she'd had. Couldn't remember what she'd been doing all afternoon, neither. That woman wasn't there, of course. Don't know where she'd got to. Her door was locked so I left her tea on that chest of drawers of hers.'

'I'd like to know what she keeps in that thing,' Phipps said, helping Cook to set out the tea-things. 'I was creeping up the stairs the other night with my shoes off, because I was a bit late coming in – and there she was, with a candle, poking about in one of the little drawers. She shut and locked it sharpish when she saw me and went back into her room so fast her candle blew out! Serves her right for being so secretive.'

'I don't trust her,' said Cook. 'Filling Miss Lucy's head with dates of old kings and queens and tales about places I never even heard of. Too much learning addles the brain. I never had much and look at me, I'm as right as rain. *I* don't forget what I've had for lunch, nor what I've been doing all afternoon. Fat chance there is of that, with all the work I've got since the mistress married again. If it hadn't been for that, we'd still have old Nanny here and she'd have seen to Miss Lucy's tea and breakfast on her little stove and you girls wouldn't be running up and down with trays.'

'I don't mind taking Miss Lucy's tray up,' Bessie declared. 'It's the other I mind. And I don't like that woman going into the nursery after Miss Lucy's been put to bed.'

'I didn't know she did that,' said Elsie, sharply.

'Well ... I've only seen her once,' Bessie admitted. 'But that's not to say she's only done it once.'

Elsie still slept in Nanny's old room, off the night nursery. It was she who woke Lucy every morning and saw that she was properly washed and dressed before Bessie brought the breakfast-tray in. It was Elsie – and sometimes Bessie – who gave Lucy her bath and put her to bed every evening, sang her old songs, told her stories. This was the time of day Lucy loved best. She was very fond of the cheerful sisters and missed her afternoon outings with Elsie.

She still went for walks when the weather was good enough, but now she went with the governess and every walk was a nature lesson or a lesson in history or local geography. She was not allowed to sit on the harbour wall and watch the boats any more, nor to run across the park like the town children, nor to feed the ducks on the pond with bits of stale bread. Those days had gone.

One night Elsie went to bed much earlier than usual with toothache. Bessie warmed her bed for her with the warming pan, after she had warmed Lucy's, and Cook heated a piece of flannel on the stove for her to hold against her swollen face.

She had no idea how long she'd been asleep when a slight sound from the night nursery woke her. The door between her room and Lucy's was always partly open, in case Lucy needed her in the night.

Elsie lay in the darkness, listening. She was almost certain that what had woken her was the unmistakable squeak of the door in Lucy's room that opened on to the day nursery. Surely Miss Lucy couldn't have got out of bed . . .? Elsie could still see the faint glow of Lucy's night-light, through the half-open door. The child wouldn't have gone into the day nursery in the dark . . . With a sigh, Elsie crept out of bed and moved quietly to the door.

What she saw made her cry out in alarm. Lucy was still curled up in bed, her long hair, braided for the night, lying across the pillow. Beside the bed stood a hooded figure in a long, loose-fitting grey garment. As the figure lifted its arm, drawing something from the folds of its gown, the flickering flame of the night-light leapt in the slight draught and glittered on a huge and shining pair of scissors.

At the sound of Elsie's cry the figure turned and vanished through the open door into the day nursery. Elsie rushed towards Lucy's bed, her heart thumping. The child had not woken, not even stirred in her sleep. Gently, Elsie pulled the covers up over her shoulders and stooped to kiss her cheek. Before going back to her own room, she went to close the door to the day nursery. As she reached it she saw Miss Dupont coming into the room from the landing, holding a candle. She was wearing the dark-green serge dress she had worn all day and her black hair was, as always, smoothly drawn back into a coil at the nape of her neck.

'Elsie!' she said, in surprise. 'Is it so late? I had no idea it was your bedtime. I lose all track of time when I am reading. I thought I heard the child cry out. Is she all right?'

'It wasn't Miss Lucy, it was me,' Elsie said, shakily. 'I came up early with toothache. Something woke me. I thought there was someone in Miss Lucy's room...'

She shivered violently. She was wearing only her nightgown.

'You're cold,' said the governess. 'Go back to bed and I will bring you something to soothe you. Oil of cloves is what you need for toothache.'

'Someone was in the room,' Elsie said, stubbornly. 'I saw someone by the bed . . .'

'A dream,' said the governess. 'A nightmare. You probably have a fever.' She put out an icy hand and touched Elsie's brow, making her shudder. 'Go back to bed,' she commanded.

Elsie went meekly back to her room, but she did not get into bed. Instead she went to the door that led to the landing and opened it an inch. The governess's room was immediately opposite, next to the schoolroom.

The governess came along the landing and put her candle on top of the mahogany chest of drawers. She took a key from the pocket in her skirt and unlocked the small middle drawer. Elsie craned her neck to see what was in it. In the flickering candlelight she saw jars and pots, small bottles, packets and twists of paper.

The governess selected what she wanted and took everything into her own room. Quietly, Elsie closed her door and climbed into bed, shivering with cold and fear and excitement.

A few minutes later there was a tap at the door and the governess came in, carrying a small glass, filled with an amber-coloured liquid. She put down her candle and took a little bottle from her pocket, giving it to Elsie.

'Drink this,' she said, offering Elsie the glass, 'then rub a little oil on your gums. It will deaden the pain.'

Elsie took the glass suspiciously. The liquid had a strange and pungent fragrance. She knew she had smelled it somewhere before. It was . . . herbs? . . . Spices? Well, if it was something Cook used, it must be all right. She drank it.

'Sleep now,' said the governess, in a low, husky voice – and before she was out of the room Elsie was almost asleep. As she drifted into unconsciousness she remembered where she had smelt the fragrance of the potion the governess had given her. It had been on Miss Lucy's breath as Elsie bent to kiss her a few moments before.

The Sunday after Elsie's 'nightmare' was bitterly cold. Lucy was kneeling on the hearthrug in front of the nursery fire playing with her dolls when the governness came into the room, carrying her workbag.

She sat down in the old rocking chair, creaking

it gently to and fro. No one had sat in that chair since Nanny left, not even Lucy. It was *Nanny's* chair and always had been – always would be. Lucy looked at the governess resentfully but Miss Dupont smiled one of her rare smiles and said, pleasantly, 'You are very cosy in here, Lucy. I hope you will not mind if I sit with you for a while? My room is cold. My fire smokes when the wind is in the east.'

Lucy said nothing. The governess opened her workbag and took out a piece of blue material. It was exactly the same colour as the new cloak Lucy had been given for Christmas. She held it up and Lucy saw, to her surprise, that it *was* a cloak – a doll's cloak, lined with satin, trimmed with white fur. She felt a little tingle of pleasure. Was this queer woman, whom she so much disliked, actually making doll's clothes for her? The dolls could certainly do with some. Nanny had not done any sewing for years. Even replacing Lucy's lost buttons and ribbons and darning her socks had been too much for her stiff old hands. Bessie had had to do it.

'You seem to take good care of your dolls,' the governess said, approvingly. 'I like that in a child. A doll is not just a plaything. It is a friend. I have one that has been with me all my life and was my mother's and grandmother's before me. Would you like to see her?'

'Yes, please,' said Lucy eagerly, scrambling to her feet. The governess put her hand into the workbag and drew out something wrapped in a piece of white silk. With great care she removed the silk and held up a little wooden doll in a white cambric petticoat. Its painted hair, black and shining, was parted in the middle, like the governess's own hair, its painted face looked bright and new, the eyes a piercing blue, the cheeks pink, the small mouth red as a cherry.

She held the doll up for Lucy to see. Then she took from the bag a red velvet dress, exactly like the one Lucy was wearing.

Lucy clapped her hands with delight. 'It's just like mine! Did you make it?'

'I did indeed,' said the governess, putting the dress on the doll. 'Now we will complete the picture.'

Once more her long thin hand went into the workbag and came out with a tiny red-and-white striped satin bag. From the bag she took, to Lucy's astonishment, a little wig of long fair hair and put it on the doll's painted head. Once more she held up the doll and said very solemnly, 'This is Lucy, my dear. Lucy, this is my dear friend, Tilly Wig.'

Lucy was enchanted – even more so when the governess took a very small soft hairbrush from the bag and began to brush the doll's long hair. As she brushed it seemed to Lucy that the hair began to grow – and as the hair grew, so did the doll. It was a foot long, now, twenty inches ... as big as Lucy's own most precious doll.

Then Lucy realized that while the doll was growing she herself was diminishing. She was no higher now than Miss Dupont's knee. The doll was above her, towering over her, its fixed smile mocking her as she grew smaller and smaller. She opened her mouth to scream but no sound came out and her mouth snapped shut again of its own accord and stayed shut. She tried to turn her head, to look away from the smiling face, but her neck was stiff. She wanted to put her hands up, to clutch at something to hold herself steady, for she could feel a curious lightness in her limbs, but her arms would not move. Nor would her legs.

The doll was on the floor beside her now, growing and growing with every long smooth stroke of the little brush. Now it was moving, first its hands and then its feet. Then it turned its head and its face was not a doll's face but a child's – Lucy's own face, looking down at her and smiling a wicked smile. Lucy's eyes opened wide in terror –

and stayed open, the lids refusing to come down again and shut out the horrible sight.

Above the doll's head the governess's face shone with the effort of brushing the lengthening hair. At the last stroke of the brush, a look of exultation came into her glittering eyes. She looked down at Lucy with a smile of triumph. Her hand ceased moving. Lucy, stiff as a stick, tumbled over as the world went black. She was a little wooden doll.

Elsie

'I've just found Miss Lucy flat out on the floor in front of the fire with her head right up against the fireguard,' Bessie said, coming downstairs, flustered and cross. 'I had to rub her arms and legs to get the life back into them. Playing on the rug with her dolls, she said and she just fell asleep. Her head was that hot . . .'

'Where was Cloth'Ilda?' asked Cook, by way of insulting Miss Dupont.

'Off for a ride on her broomstick, the old witch,' said Phipps, grinning.

'I don't know where she is,' Bessie said. 'I banged on her door and called loud enough. If she wants her tea cold, she can have it cold, for all I care!'

'That's funny,' Elsie said. 'I saw Miss Lucy in the back hall not ten minutes ago. Miss Dupont was going up the back stairs. I thought they'd just come in from the garden, but Miss Lucy had no

coat on. Went upstairs without a word, she did. Didn't even look at me.'

'That woman's a bad influence,' Cook said. 'She's driving that child into a decline with all that book learning. There'll be trouble, you mark my words. There'll be trouble.'

The only person who seemed to be pleased with Lucy's progress was Dr Marchbanks. He sent for her to come down to the drawing-room at least once a week and questioned her about her lessons, examining her exercise books with care.

'The child is doing remarkably well,' he said one day. 'I congratulate you, Mademoiselle.' (No one else called the governess 'Mademoiselle', but the doctor always did.) 'I heard in France that you had your own methods of instructing the young and that they were very successful. You certainly seem to have achieved great things in the short time you have been teaching Lucy.'

'Thank you, sir,' said the governess, with a small tight smile. 'My methods have sometimes been criticised for being too unusual, but the results, I think, are gratifying.'

'Very,' agreed Dr Marchbanks. 'Carry on with the good work.'

'Are you sure Lucy isn't doing *too* much for one so young?' asked Lucy's mother, anxiously. 'She

Elsie

'I've just found Miss Lucy flat out on the floor in front of the fire with her head right up against the fireguard,' Bessie said, coming downstairs, flustered and cross. 'I had to rub her arms and legs to get the life back into them. Playing on the rug with her dolls, she said and she just fell asleep. Her head was that hot...'

'Where was Cloth'Ilda?' asked Cook, by way of insulting Miss Dupont.

'Off for a ride on her broomstick, the old witch,' said Phipps, grinning.

'I don't know where she is,' Bessie said. 'I banged on her door and called loud enough. If she wants her tea cold, she can have it cold, for all I care!'

'That's funny,' Elsie said. 'I saw Miss Lucy in the back hall not ten minutes ago. Miss Dupont was going up the back stairs. I thought they'd just come in from the garden, but Miss Lucy had no

coat on. Went upstairs without a word, she did. Didn't even look at me.'

'That woman's a bad influence,' Cook said. 'She's driving that child into a decline with all that book learning. There'll be trouble, you mark my words.. There'll be trouble.'

The only person who seemed to be pleased with Lucy's progress was Dr Marchbanks. He sent for her to come down to the drawing-room at least once a week and questioned her about her lessons, examining her exercise books with care.

'The child is doing remarkably well,' he said one day. 'I congratulate you, Mademoiselle.' (No one else called the governess 'Mademoiselle', but the doctor always did.) 'I heard in France that you had your own methods of instructing the young and that they were very successful. You certainly seem to have achieved great things in the short time you have been teaching Lucy.'

'Thank you, sir,' said the governess, with a small tight smile. 'My methods have sometimes been criticised for being too unusual, but the results, I think, are gratifying.'

'Very,' agreed Dr Marchbanks. 'Carry on with the good work.'

'Are you sure Lucy isn't doing *too* much for one so young?' asked Lucy's mother, anxiously. 'She

Elsie

'I've just found Miss Lucy flat out on the floor in front of the fire with her head right up against the fireguard,' Bessie said, coming downstairs, flustered and cross. 'I had to rub her arms and legs to get the life back into them. Playing on the rug with her dolls, she said and she just fell asleep. Her head was that hot . . .'

'Where was Cloth'Ilda?' asked Cook, by way of insulting Miss Dupont.

'Off for a ride on her broomstick, the old witch,' said Phipps, grinning.

'I don't know where she is,' Bessie said. 'I banged on her door and called loud enough. If she wants her tea cold, she can have it cold, for all I care!'

'That's funny,' Elsie said. 'I saw Miss Lucy in the back hall not ten minutes ago. Miss Dupont was going up the back stairs. I thought they'd just come in from the garden, but Miss Lucy had no

coat on. Went upstairs without a word, she did. Didn't even look at me.'

'That woman's a bad influence,' Cook said. 'She's driving that child into a decline with all that book learning. There'll be trouble, you mark my words.. There'll be trouble.'

The only person who seemed to be pleased with Lucy's progress was Dr Marchbanks. He sent for her to come down to the drawing-room at least once a week and questioned her about her lessons, examining her exercise books with care.

'The child is doing remarkably well,' he said one day. 'I congratulate you, Mademoiselle.' (No one else called the governess 'Mademoiselle', but the doctor always did.) 'I heard in France that you had your own methods of instructing the young and that they were very successful. You certainly seem to have achieved great things in the short time you have been teaching Lucy.'

'Thank you, sir,' said the governess, with a small tight smile. 'My methods have sometimes been criticised for being too unusual, but the results, I think, are gratifying.'

'Very,' agreed Dr Marchbanks. 'Carry on with the good work.'

'Are you sure Lucy isn't doing *too* much for one so young?' asked Lucy's mother, anxiously. 'She

passed me on the landing the other afternoon and went straight upstairs without taking any notice of me, even when I spoke to her. It was as though she neither saw nor heard me.'

'I don't remember that, Mama,' said Lucy, surprised. 'When was it?'

'It was last Sunday afternoon,' said her mother, looking a little hurt. 'I was on my way down to tea. I asked you if you would like to come and have tea in the drawing-room as a special treat.'

Lucy put her hand to her head. 'Sunday ...' she said. 'That was the day I had the funny dream...'

'What funny dream?' asked Elsie. She was putting Lucy to bed and Lucy had just told her what her mother had said.

'I dreamed Miss Dupont was dressing a doll,' said Lucy. 'And the doll looked like me. And then I dreamed that I *was* the doll and the dream wasn't funny any more. It was horrid.'

A few days later, Elsie found Lucy sitting on her bed, shivering and holding her head in her hands.

'What is it, my love?' she asked, putting her arm round the child.

'I had that dream again,' Lucy said. 'Only Miss

Dupont wasn't in it this time. It was just me and I was a doll. I woke up all stiff, like when Bessie found me by the fire the other day.'

'Were you on the hearthrug again?' asked Elsie. The child was over-tired ... Maybe the heat of the fire had sent her to sleep.

'No. I was here, on my bed. Only I don't remember coming to lie down.'

'Well, come and have your lunch,' said Elsie, soothingly. 'You'll feel better then.'

Lucy had her 'bad dream' several times during the weeks that followed. Elsie was the only person she told. At first Elsie kept the knowledge to herself but she became so worried about Lucy's increasing strangeness that she told first Bessie and then Phipps and Cook.

'She says she wakes up all stiff and her head hurts,' Elsie said. 'It's not natural for a child to wake up like that after a little nap.'

'She only has this dream in the daytime, then?' asked Phipps.

'Yes, I think so. She never said anything about having it at night. She's always perfectly all right when I go to wake her in the morning.'

'Hmm,' said Phipps. 'Sounds fishy to me.'

'It's that woman,' declared Cook. 'She's

putting ideas in the child's head. I've heard of such things. Hypnotism, that's what it's called. Either that or she's giving her something that's making her sleep too sound. Though why she should want the child to sleep in the daytime is more than I can fathom.'

'Something to make her sleep...' Elsie said, slowly. 'She gave me something to make me sleep when I had toothache that time – and I'm sure she gave Miss Lucy something, too ... but Miss Lucy didn't have a bad dream that night. I was the one who had the nightmare – and that was before I had the sleeping draught.'

She went over and over it in her mind, then with Bessie and the others.

'I don't reckon you *were* dreaming,' Cook said. 'I reckon it was Cloth'Ilda about to do Miss Lucy a mischief.'

'Cut off her hair,' said Bessie. 'Like Samson and Delilah. Miss Lucy's got lovely hair. She could be jealous, the old crow.'

'Cut off her hair!' cried Elsie. 'That's it! That's what she was going to do. She did cut some off, a few days later. I remember saying to Miss Lucy when I was brushing it that it seemed shorter and she said Miss Dupont had given her a trim because it looked a bit ragged.'

'There you are!' said Phipps triumphantly. 'I always said she was a witch. Witches like to get hold of people's hair to put spells on them.'

During the spring and summer of that terrible year, all the servants in the house on the Esplanade kept watch on the dark, secretive governess and the pale, frightened child who was in her charge. As week followed week Lucy grew more silent, more nervous, more withdrawn. She started at the slightest unexpected sound, her blue eyes darkening with fear. She no longer played with her dolls, but spent her free time sitting on the window-seat in the nursery, staring out across the bay.

In the early weeks, when fires were still being lit every morning, Bessie would sometimes make a low fire in the schoolroom and forget to fill the coal scuttle, so as to give herself an excuse for going in later on.

'I can't make it out,' she said, after one of these spying trips 'She's not like any teacher I ever had. She's just sitting there watching Miss Lucy – and Miss Lucy, with her head down, scribbling away as if her life depended on it. Once when I went in they were just sitting there staring at one another. Not a word said between them.'

'There you are!' cried Cook, triumphantly. 'I told you so. She's got that child in her power, the old witch!'

Elsie, on an errand for Cook one afternoon in early summer, thought she would come out of town by way of Castle Walk and Quay Street and pay a quick visit to her mother.

As she hurried along by the castle, she was a little put out to see the governess and Lucy sitting on the iron seat by the castle wall. From that seat there was a clear view straight down Quay Street to the harbour. Elsie's house was just a little way down the hill on the right – what if she were seen going into the house? The governess was sitting with head slightly bent, reading, her grey-gloved hands holding the book fairly close to her face. Lucy was sitting at the other end of the seat.

She was wearing a pale-blue silk dress and a wide-brimmed hat with long blue ribbons at the back. Her hands, in their white cotton gloves, were folded in her lap and she was staring straight in front of her.

Elsie passed them as far away as possible, hoping her shadow would not fall on Miss Dupont's book. The governess did not look up and Lucy gave not the slightest sign that she had seen anyone go by. Elsie hurried down the hill towards the harbour, looking over her shoulder every few steps. The governess was still engrossed in her book and Lucy still sat motionless beside her. Elsie's mother always had the front door open on fine days. Elsie ran up the steps and into the house, thankful to be out of sight.

'They've been up there over an hour,' Elsie's mother said, when she mentioned the governess and Lucy. 'She's had her nose stuck in a book and Miss Lucy hasn't moved an inch since she sat down. It's unnatural, that's what it is, for a child to sit so still.'

'Go to the door, Willie, and see if the lady and the little girl are still on the seat up the hill,' Elsie said to one of her younger brothers some ten minutes later. 'Don't let them see you looking, mind.'

There was no need for him to be careful. The seat was empty. The governess and Lucy were nowhere to be seen.

When Elsie got back to the house on the Esplanade she found Lucy lying on her bed, apparently just waking up from a deep sleep. Her blue silk dress was not crumpled, she was still wearing her white gloves, and her straw hat was on the floor by the door.

'My head hurts,' she moaned, sitting up. 'It feels as though someone's been pulling my hair. And I had that horrible dream again ... I dreamed I was a doll...'

'Just you let me catch the old witch pulling Miss Lucy's hair and I'll give her what for,' said Bessie, indignantly. 'The idea!'

Thoughtfully, Elsie began to prepare Lucy's tea-tray. She had hurried from her mother's house as soon as she knew it was safe to go, and as she left the harbour and began the long climb up to the Esplanade, she had seen the governess and Lucy ahead of her on the hill. By the time they reached the house, she had almost caught up with them. They were halfway up the short flight of steps to the garden door as she reached the steps that led down to the basement. They could not have gone up the back stairs more than a minute before she did, yet when she reached her room she had seen, through the half-open inner door, Miss Lucy lying on her bed, seemingly just waking up. How was it possible?

As the weeks went by Elsie was no nearer solving the mystery. Lucy's 'bad dream' became more frequent, and so did her strange, unseeing silences.

One chilly afternoon in September Dr Marchbanks was in the hall with two gentlemen who were on the point of leaving when Miss Dupont and Lucy came in at the garden door at the far end of the hall.

He called out to them 'Ah! Mademoiselle, Lucy. Do not go upstairs for a moment. Come into the drawing-room. Dr Lovelace and Dr Charlton would be most interested to learn the results of your teaching methods, Mademoiselle.'

With great reluctance the governess shepherded Lucy down the hall and into the drawing-room. The three doctors followed her in. Dr Lovelace spoke to Lucy, asking her if she had enjoyed her walk.

She did not answer him, nor give any sign that she had heard.

'Is the child deaf?' he asked.

'No – no – ' Dr Marchbanks assured him. 'A little shy, maybe. She is not used to meeting people. Lucy, tell me what you have been studying today.'

Again Lucy made no answer. She stood beside the governess staring straight ahead of her.

'Lucy!' said Dr Marchbanks, impatiently. 'Tell these gentlemen what you have learned today.'

Still no answer. There were other visitors in the room, chatting with Lucy's mother. They all fell silent, looking at Lucy. She took no notice of them. Her mother stood up and came towards her, but before she reached her she stopped, saying in a puzzled voice, 'Lucy – are you unwell?' Lucy ignored her.

Elsie had been sent for to make up the fire. She knelt by the hearth, tongs in hand, watching Lucy. She had seen her like this so many times before...

'Answer me, Lucy,' Dr Marchbanks said, exasperated by Lucy's silence. 'What have you been doing today?'

'If I may interrupt, sir,' said the governess, 'The child has been concentrating on what I have been teaching her. We have had a most instructive walk. It is part of my way of teaching that she should empty her mind of everything save what I want her to remember. If you will allow me, I will take her upstairs and when she has rested – in about five or ten minutes – I will bring her down again with the work she did this morning.'

Dr Charlton suddenly snapped his fingers almost under Lucy's nose. She did not even blink.

'Extraordinary!' he said. Then, as the governess and Lucy went out of the room, he added in a low voice to Dr Lovelace, 'It's my opinion that the child is mesmerized. She is in a hypnotic trance.'

Elsie, mending the fire, heard him. She put the tongs and coal-scuttle back in their places and went quickly out of the room.

As she crept up the back stairs she could hear, ahead of her, the light footsteps of Miss Dupont and Lucy. When she reached the last flight she moved cautiously towards the landing. Miss Dupont was standing with her back to the stairs, Lucy motionless beside her.

Elsie saw her raise her hand and snatch the blue velvet hat from Lucy's head. Then with her other hand, she gathered up Lucy's long fair hair and pulled it, hard.

Elsie pushed her fist into her mouth to stop herself crying out. There was a tearing sound as Lucy's hair came off in the governess's hand – and Lucy disappeared. Something fell to the floor at the governess's feet. It was a little wooden doll. She bent and picked it up, pushing it into the embroidered workbag she so often carried about with her. Elsie flattened herself against the stair wall as the governess turned towards the chest of drawers. There was the sound of a small drawer sliding out and sliding back and a key turned in the lock. Then the governess crossed the landing and went into the nursery, carrying Lucy's blue velvet hat.

Elsie stumbled into Nanny's old room in a state of shock. The inner door was ajar. She heard the familiar squeak of the other night nursery door as it was opened. A second later it squealed shut. Elsie waited a moment to be sure the governess had gone, then crept to the inner door of her own room. Fearfully she peeped into the night nursery. Lucy's hat was on the floor, where the governess had flung it. Lucy was lying on the bed in her outdoor things, moaning softly and holding her head.

For days Elsie could not bring herself to tell anyone what she had seen. Then, one afternoon while Lucy and the governess were out, she told her sister. Bessie, she knew, would not tell her she had imagined it.

Bessie was silent for a long time. Then she said, slowly, 'That's not mesmerism nor hypnotism – or whatever you call it. That's plain old-fashioned witchcraft.'

'What can we *do*?' asked Elsie.

'Well, for a start, we'll have to get hold of that doll,' Bessie said, firmly.

'But it's in the chest of drawers. The drawer's locked.'

'Anybody can tell you ain't been in service long,' Bessie said, scornfully. 'A house like this is full of keys. There's a big bunch of 'em down in the boot room. There's sure to be one that fits.'

Bessie was right. After a nerve-racking five minutes of trial and error, they found a key that fitted the locks of the small drawers at the top of the chest.

Trembling, Elsie pulled the first drawer open. It was full of books. Disappointed, she closed it, without bothering to look at them.

'I know what's in the middle one,' she said. 'Pots and bottles.'

'Let's have a look,' begged Bessie. Elsie opened the drawer. There were the packets, bottles and jars she had seen the night she had toothache; some with strange-sounding names on the labels, others with familiar ones, like bergamot and rosemary, cloves and peppermint.

'I wish I knew what she put in that sleeping draught,' Elsie said. 'I'd make one up for her, double strong.'

She opened the third drawer – with a little tingle of excitement she saw that it contained the embroidered workbag. Carefully she pulled it out and opened it.

There was no doll.

Bessie put her hand into the bag and pulled out a bit of blue silk.

'Well, I never!' she said. 'Here's a little dress just like Miss Lucy's blue! And look, here's her red velvet – and her white muslin. Phipps *said* she'd seen that woman sewing bits of stuff no bigger than a pocket handkerchief ... What does it mean?'

'Put it back,' Elsie said, in a voice full of fear. 'We've got to go and look in the nursery.'

'I'm supposed to be sorting out the linen,' Bessie reminded her. 'There'll be a nice fuss in the morning when the washerwoman comes, if it's not done.'

'This won't take a minute,' Elsie said, and went into her room. After a moment's hesitation, Bessie followed her. She found her sister by the inner door, staring into the night nursery.

The room was as neat and tidy as it should be. Nothing was out of place – but on the bed, dressed in Lucy's grey coat and red velvet bonnet, lay a little wooden doll.

'Grab hold of it and chuck it on the fire!' cried Bessie, starting forward.

Elsie caught at her arm. 'No! Don't you see? It's not really a doll. It's Miss Lucy!'

CHAPTER EIGHT

Bessie

It took Bessie some time to understand. 'You mean she turns Miss Lucy into a doll and the doll into Miss Lucy?' she said, at last.

'Not really into Miss Lucy,' said Elsie. 'Into someone – some Thing – that looks like her. Something that walks when she tells it, sits when she tells it, but never says a word. Remember that day we watched Miss Lucy walking in the garden by herself? She went round and round the big rose bed in the middle like one of those toys you wind up and set going. Then that woman went out and took hold of her and brought her back to the house. Remember?'

Bessie nodded. 'Yes. And that wasn't Miss Lucy ... that was the doll, magicked up to look like her?'

'I think so.'

'Well, how are we going to stop her?'

'I don't know,' Elsie said. 'But we'll find a way.

And soon, before Miss Lucy goes right out of her mind.'

'Best way would be to turn that old witch into a doll herself,' Bessie declared. 'I wonder how she does it?'

Elsie found out how, the following Sunday. She went into the nursery with the tea-tray and found Lucy playing with her dolls for once, instead of staring out of the window. At least, she was playing with one doll, the one she had been given last Christmas. It had long, coarse hair. Lucy was brushing it with her own hairbrush.

'It's no use,' she sighed, as Elsie put the tray down. 'I expect you have to use the special little brush.'

'What for?' asked Elsie.

'To make it grow, of course. Miss Dupont's doll grew and grew when she brushed its hair. And the hair grew and grew, too. Only it wasn't really the doll's hair, it was mine. The bit she cut off. She made it into a wig for the doll.'

She frowned. 'I don't think she did really,' she said. 'I think I just dreamed it.'

'So that's it!' said Bessie, when Elsie told her. 'What special brush, I wonder? And how do we get hold of it?'

'There was a little brush in that workbag,' said Elsie. 'Didn't you see it? Small and soft, it was – like a baby's hairbrush.'

'Well, you've still got that key. You get hold of the brush, next time she's out.'

'What use is that?' asked Elsie. 'We've got to have a wig to brush with it.'

The wig was a problem. How were they going to cut off some of the governess's hair without her knowing? Then Bessie had a brainwave. As housemaid she had to go into the governess's room every day to clean and tidy. On the dressing-table was a china hair tidy into which Miss Dupont put all the hair that came out in her comb and brush. Bessie began to collect it, putting it carefully into a little cotton bag in the pocket of her apron. Every evening she or Elsie threaded a fine needle with the long dark strands and stitched them to a little cotton cap which Elsie had made.

'This is going to take *years*,' Bessie sighed, untangling a knot of hair one evening.

'We don't have to leave the hairs long,' said Elsie. 'We can cut them into pieces. Her hair is only down to her shoulders, not down to her waist like Miss Lucy's.'

'It's going to be a thin wig,' Bessie said, 'whichever way we do it.'

The year was drawing to an end. The next year would bring great changes to the house on the Esplanade. Already there were plans for redecorating and refurbishing the nursery. By the spring there would be a new Nanny in old Nanny's room, a new baby in the night nursery. Elsie would be back up in the attic with Bessie, and Lucy would be in the room on the other side of the landing, next to the governess – the room her father had slept in when he was a boy. It would be much more difficult for Elsie to keep an eye on her there.

Miss Dupont was going to France for a week at Christmas.

In November she went to a dressmaker near the harbour and had two new dresses made; one for day and one for evening wear. The day dress was of rough green serge, rather like the one she usually wore. This was Elsie's chance. She knew the dressmaker well and went to her house to beg bits of material.

'Mother wants to make a new rag rug,' she said.

Among the scraps the dressmaker gave her were pieces of the green serge she had used for Miss Dupont's dress.

It was easy for Elsie to make a copy of the dress. The style was simple, there were no trimmings, no fussy bits and pieces – just a long-sleeved dress with a high neckline, a tight waist and a long, full skirt. She guessed the size. She could not bring herself to go to the drawer on the landing again and look for the doll. There would be time enough for that when everything was prepared . . .

The dress was made, the wig was almost completed, though the hair on it was sparse. All Bessie and Elsie needed now was the opportunity to try out the governess's magic.

The opportunity came the very day that the governess was due to go away. Dr Lovelace's wife and daughters invited Lucy to a party in their house, a little farther up the Esplanade. Elsie took her there and came back to find Miss Dupont in the kitchen, about to go out. Under her black coat she was wearing her new green dress.

'I shall not be in for tea,' she said. 'I have some shopping of my own to do and a very important task to perform for Mrs Marchbanks. I shall take tea in the Grand Hotel. I shall return to the house to rest for an hour before I catch the train to London.'

'She's gone to the jeweller in the High Street to collect Mrs Marchbanks's pearl necklace,' Phipps said. 'It's been re-strung. Don't know why she didn't ask *me* to fetch it. I wouldn't trust that old witch with a string of wooden beads.'

Elsie and Bessie looked at each other. This was their chance.

As soon as they could, they went up to the nursery landing. With trembling fingers Elsie opened the drawer where the workbag was kept, her heart thumping for fear it was not there. It was – and the doll was inside it.

A feeling of revulsion came over her as she took it out and looked at it, yet there was nothing sinister in its appearance. Its painted face was expressionless, its blue eyes blank. She dressed it in the green serge dress and carefully fitted the little wig over its shiny black head. Then she took the tiny brush from the bag, put the bag back in its place and locked the drawer. It was most unlikely that the governess would go to the drawer as soon as she returned from town.

Elsie and Bessie took it in turns to watch out for the governess. They knew that they must begin their work on the doll as soon as she returned, that they must be quick in case she had some powerful magic that she could invoke as soon as she realised something was wrong.

Lucy was to be collected at six o'clock. By half past five the governess had still not returned and Elsie was almost sick with anxiety.

'Do it *now*,' Bessie urged her. 'What does it matter where she is when it happens?'

'What if it doesn't happen? What if I don't do it right?' asked Elsie. 'How shall we know, if we don't know where she is?'

'But it's my night off,' protested Bessie.

'What must be done must be done,' said Elsie firmly.

At twenty to six Miss Dupont came in by the garden door and, instead of going to the drawing-room with Mrs Marchbank's pearl necklace, she went straight up to her room.

For once, she left her bedroom door open. Elsie had raced upstairs as soon as she saw the governess's black boots and long skirts go past the high window in the basement kitchen. She was standing in her room, her door open a crack. She watched Miss Dupont take off her hat and coat and stand before her wardrobe mirror. She was wearing Mrs Marchbanks's pearls.

With trembling hands Elsie picked up the doll and began brushing at the thin wig. Some of the inexpertly sewn hairs came out but those that were left began to grow ... and grow ...

Across the landing the governess suddenly put her hand to her head. Elsie brushed faster, terrified that the spell would not begin to work before she was discovered. Miss Dupont swayed and sat down heavily on the edge of her bed.

Then Elsie realised that the doll was growing – still a doll, still stiff and wooden in her hands, but bigger, much bigger. Feeling a little sick she stood it on the floor and knelt beside it, holding it steady with one hand while she went on with the rhythmic brushing. From across the landing came a choking cry. The governess was leaning against her door-frame, holding her head in both hands. She seemed to have grown smaller.

Bessie came up the back stairs with a hod of coal for the nursery fire. She passed Miss Dupont's door without looking that way. The governess gave no sign that she had seen Bessie. She was staring across the landing at the door of Elsie's room, her black eyes wild, her face distorted in a snarl of rage. Gasping and choking, she staggered on to the landing. Watching her, the terrified Elsie brushed faster, but the governess turned towards the chest of drawers, reaching up and fumbling at the drawer where she kept the workbag. Elsie had locked it and the governess's keys were not in the pocket of her new green gown.

With a cry of despair the fast-shrinking governess turned to go back to her room.

By now Bessie had joined Elsie. She looked in

round-eyed wonder at the doll, which was now as tall as Miss Lucy, a strange little creature, like a miniature Miss Dupont, its blue eyes already darkening, its face less doll-like. Suddenly it blinked and fluttered its hands. Elsie gave a shriek of terror and dropped the brush. Bessie snatched it up and went on brushing the thin hair.

Then from across the landing came a terrible cry. On hands and knees Elsie opened the door a little wider. The governess lay on the landing, her eyes wide open, her mouth tight shut.

Elsie gave a great sob. 'Oh, Bess ... what have we done?'

'We're not done yet,' said Bessie, grimly, still brushing the wispy hair. The creature was as tall as she was now. It offered no resistance when she pushed it down on to a chair.

The governess's pebble-hard eyes were fixed on Elsie's face. The look of hatred in them filled her with fear. Trembling, she watched as the governess grew smaller and smaller. Then, suddenly, the black eyes were bright blue and blank, and the governess was a doll.

With a shout of joy and relief, Elsie rushed on to the landing and picked up the harmless little doll. It was the work of a moment to unlock the drawer, open the workbag, thrust the doll inside it and lock the drawer again.

Then she hurried out to collect Miss Lucy from the party, leaving Bessie to deal with the doll that had become the governess.

Bessie led the doll-governess across the landing and into Miss Dupont's room. She sat her on the bed, coiled her wispy hair into a knot and secured it with hairpins. Then she rammed Miss Dupont's black hat on her head, told her to stand up and folded her into the long black coat. It was uncanny to see someone who looked so like the hateful governess and yet was so different. The doll-governess said nothing, did not even look at Bessie, yet she obeyed her every command. Miss Dupont's hold-all was packed ready for her journey. Her bag and gloves were on the dressing-table. Bessie put the gloves on the doll-governess's unresisting hands – really, it was worse than dressing Miss Lucy, she thought. A little nervously she picked up the handbag and looked in it. All the tickets and documents Miss Dupont would need for her trip to France were there, together with a note of the times of trains and the cross-channel steamer, also the name of the hotel where she was supposed to be staying in London. There was

French and English money, too – and at the bottom of the bag a bunch of keys.

Bessie's first thought had been simply to get the doll-governess out of the house before anyone knew she was there, but now she had a better idea.

She waited till Elsie came back with Lucy and then went into the nursery. Lucy was chattering and laughing excitedly. It was nearly a year since Bessie had seen her so happy.

Taking Elsie aside Bessie whispered, 'I'm going to the station. Go down and make sure there's no one about.'

'What are you whispering for?' asked Lucy.

'Secrets,' said Bessie.

'Is it something nice?'

'Oh, yes, very nice. You'll think so, I'm sure, when you find out.'

'Oh, I know, I know,' cried Lucy, clapping her hands. 'It's a surprise for me, isn't it?'

'It's a surprise for everyone,' said Bessie and went to put on her hat and coat.

She and Elsie managed to get the doll-governess out of the house unseen. By now the blinds had been drawn in the kitchen so no one would see two sets of feet go by instead of one.

Back in the house, Elsie heard Mrs Marchbanks in the hall saying, 'Phipps, is Miss Dupont returned from town yet?'

'I don't think so, madam,' said Phipps. 'Would you like me to go up and see?'

'No ... no ...' said her mistress. 'But I hope she won't be too long. The doctor and I have a dinner engagement this evening and I want to wear my pearls.'

The pearls! Elsie had forgotten all about them. She ran upstairs and unlocked the drawer where she had put the doll. Round its neck was a necklace of tiny pearls.

Elsie stared at the doll, not knowing what to do. The necklace was useless now, too small even to be used as a bracelet.

She made a movement to push the doll back into the bag. The light of her candle caught its shining hair, its face – and it seemed to her that its expression changed. The eyes were full of hatred, the mouth a snarl – the face of the governess as she lay on the landing looking at Elsie. Another flicker of the candleflame and all was as it should be, the doll was just a doll.

Shuddering, Elsie drew from her apron pocket the little blue cotton bag she had made for Bessie to collect Miss Dupont's hair in and pulled it over the doll's head, tying the drawstring with many knots, as tight as she could make them. Then she put the doll back in the drawer, locked it and went into her room. With trembling hands she opened her window and flung the key out into the darkness of the winter night.

PART THREE

Quay Street:
1987

CHAPTER NINE

Time ...

Linda gave a long sigh. 'So that was it...'

'That was it,' said Gran. 'And now you know.'

'But what did Bessie ... Great-aunt Bessie *do* with her?' asked Angie.

'Took her to the station of course, and put her on the train,' Gran said. 'She had her tickets.'

'I wonder what happened to her?'

'We'll never know. We never heard of her again.'

'It's creepy.' Linda shuddered.

'No more creepy than what you and Joanna did,' Gran said. 'The problem now is, what are we going to do about the real Miss Dupont – Tilda, as you call her.'

'Is she *really* that awful governess?' asked Angie, hardly able to believe it.

'Oh yes,' said Gran, firmly. 'She is. I saw her face quite clearly from the window. There's no mistaking it.'

She sighed. 'It was stupid of me not to remember that the wig was in the bag when I locked the doll in the drawer, but I never gave it a thought. I was so glad to be rid of her. To think the chest of drawers has been up on the landing all these years. Nobody ever thought to look in it – not while I was in service there, anyway. It belonged to Miss Dupont, though we all knew she'd never come back for it. Of course, Dr Marchbanks thought she'd made off with Mrs Marchbanks's pearls. She was seen wearing them by two of Mrs Marchbanks's friends, when she had tea in the Grand Hotel that day. They were quite valuable. Even more valuable now, I suppose.'

'And Samantha's gone to the disco in them,' murmured Linda.

Gran didn't seem to hear her. She was thinking about Miss Lucy.

'I don't think Dr Marchbanks ever cared much for Miss Lucy,' she said. 'He packed her off to boarding school soon after Master Henry was born, though she wouldn't have been too much for the new Nanny to manage. Still, he was strict with Master Henry, too. The poor boy didn't have an easy time of it. He went off to Canada as soon as he was old enough and never came back till after his father died. There was nothing for him here, of course. The house belonged to Miss

Lucy – left in trust for her by her father, Captain Tregoran. Whatever he might have wanted, there was no way the doctor could alter that. Master Henry brought his daughter, Janet, with him when he came over after his father's funeral. She came back a year or two later and she's been with Miss Lucy ever since. The house will be hers eventually, I suppose. It'll take a lot of keeping up, a big place like that. I hope Miss Lucy hasn't been finding it difficult to manage, with everything so expensive nowadays... I cannot think what else would make her sell that chest of drawers. It's a nice piece – worth quite a bit, I expect.'

'She wouldn't get much from Mr Baldock,' Angie said.

'Perhaps we ought to try and get the pearl necklace back,' Linda suggested. 'If it's worth a lot of money?'

Gran looked at her. 'Doesn't matter how much it's worth, it's no use to Miss Lucy now,' she said, sadly.

'Why not?' asked Angie, but it was Linda who answered her, filled with the awful realisation of what she and Joanna had done.

'Because it was the wig made out of Miss Lucy's hair we put on the doll – which means that if the doll has turned into a person, then Miss Lucy's turned into a doll.'

The girls slept very little that night. Supper had been late because of Gran's tale of long ago. Angie's mother had wanted to interrupt her but Angie's father had said, 'Leave the old girl alone. She's enjoying herself.'

After supper Gran had asked Linda to fetch her the old workbag, but when Linda went to find it, it was nowhere to be seen

'I bet Joanna has taken it,' she said. 'It was just inside the front door. She did ask me for it – she said Tilda wanted it, but I said she couldn't have it.'

Gran looked worried. 'It wasn't the bag she wanted,' she said. 'It was the brush. I don't like the sound of that.'

The girls talked in whispers long after Linda's parents had gone to bed – Linda's mother called out to them once, but it was impossible to keep silent for long.

'All we've got to do,' said Angie, 'is pull Tilly's wig off.'

Linda shivered. 'I couldn't – it would be horrible.' Then she added, 'Tilly Wig ... wasn't that what she called her doll? No wonder she was so cross when you called her Tilly. She must have thought you knew about her.'

'Well, I didn't,' said Angie, 'but I do now – and if you're too squeamish to grab her by the hair, *I'm* not!'

At one o'clock they heard Samantha come home, thoughtlessly shouting her goodbyes to the friends who had accompanied her and slamming the front door. That set them off on a new topic – how to get the pearl necklace for Miss Lucy.

'We'd better try and get some sleep,' Linda yawned, some time later. 'Shall I draw the curtains?'

She went to the window. 'All the lights are on in Joanna's house,' she said. 'I wonder what's going on?'

'She was in my room!' Samantha said, indignantly. 'I hadn't been in bed all that long. I left my door open to get a bit of air through because it was so hot, so I didn't hear her come in. I opened my eyes and there she was, standing by the bed with the kitchen scissors in her hand! I could have been killed! She's mad!'

There had been a great rumpus over at Joanna's house in the night. Samantha's screams had sent Mrs Porter, the neighbour, hurrying in.

Joanna had been woken from a deep sleep and seemed to be in a daze. Samantha was hysterical, and Tilda – Tilda was in bed, apparently quite unaware that anything was wrong.

'You must have been dreaming, dear,' said Mrs Porter, soothingly, when Samantha had calmed down a little.

'Of course I wasn't dreaming! She was there! She dropped the scissors on the floor by the bed. They're still here – look – she's mad, I tell you. She's got to go.'

'We can't turn her out in the middle of the night,' said Mrs Porter. 'Whatever would your mother say? Be reasonable, dear.'

'Well, if she doesn't go, I will,' declared Samantha, beginning to collect garments. 'I'll go to Emma's. Her mother won't mind.'

There was no stopping her. Five minutes later she was dressed and out of the house.

She came to Linda's house soon after ten on Sunday morning, asking if she and Angie knew where Joanna and Tilda had gone. They were not in the house. They had not been there when Mrs Porter went in first thing to make sure everything was all right. No one knew when or where they had gone.

'She wasn't trying to kill Sam, of course,' Linda

said, when Samantha had gone. 'She was trying to cut her hair.'

'Whatever for?' asked Angie. 'She couldn't have made it into a wig – not one big enough to fit her now. Anyway, what's wrong with the one she's got?'

'It's the wrong colour. Samantha's hair is dark, like hers was. Besides, Sam's taller than Miss Lucy was when the wig was made. Her hair would make Tilda look more ... grown-up. Not as queer.'

Linda had a mental picture of Tilda's dark, evil face just after Angie had called her 'Tilly', the sallow skin and black brows incongruous under the pale hair.

'That's why she wanted the brush,' she said. 'To make the hair grow, so she could grow too.'

Angie sniffed. She was still finding it hard to believe that all these incredible things had really happened. At the back of her mind was the thought that it would all turn out to be some sort of practical joke. Still, if Gran and Linda wanted her to go along with it, she would.

'Why can't Tilda just cut the fair wig and put a dark one on top?' she suggested. 'You can buy wigs in the hairdressers...'

'She'd still look queer,' Linda said. 'She wouldn't be any taller than she is now.'

They were sitting on Angie's front doorstep. Gran came to the door and said, 'Angie, go and see if you can find out who sold that chest of drawers to Mr Baldock. I want to know if it was Miss Lucy or her niece.'

'Who wants to know?' Mr Baldock asked, suspiciously, when Angie went through his yard and asked him. 'I don't make a habit of tellin' people where I get things. Besides, it's Sunday. I don't do business on a Sunday.'

'We know where you got it,' Angie said. 'It was from a house on the Esplanade. I'll tell you which one, if you like. My Gran was in service there. She just wants to know *who sold it to you*. Was it Miss Tregoran?'

Mr Baldock shook his head. 'Nope. The other one. There, that's all I'm saying.'

'I've got to go to the Esplanade,' Gran said. 'There's no two ways about it. I've got to find out what's happened to Miss Lucy. But first I must go and have a word with Mr Baldock. Come up the hill with me, you two. I'm not as nippy on the cobbles as I was when I was your age.'

'Nobby Baldock,' she said, when Mr Baldock opened his back door. 'I knew you when you were in short trousers. Before, even. So I want the truth

126

about that chest of drawers. None of your yarns, now.'

'All right ... all right...' grumbled Mr Baldock. 'The old lady's turning the top and bottom of the house into flats, like most of 'em already are, up there. Nobody can afford them big places these days. She got rid of all the furniture and stuff a couple of weeks ago. I did quite well out of it. Only she wouldn't let anybody touch that chest of drawers. Said it didn't belong to her by rights. I offered her good money for it, but she wouldn't budge.

Then, last Friday evenin', the other one got me on the 'phone and said her auntie had gone into a nursing home up the road and if I wanted the chest of drawers I was to come with a couple of strong lads, ten o'clock sharp Saturday morning. She was going out herself at eleven, she said, to catch a train. There! That satisfy you?'

'More or less,' said Gran. 'Just one more thing. Were the drawers still locked? Was the chest still full of stuff?'

'Locks is no problem,' said Mr Baldock. 'I got keys. One of my lads unlocked a couple of the drawers. Books, mostly, and old clothes. Looked as if they came out of the ark, most of 'em.' He grinned. 'Yours, was it? Young Angie said you used to work there one time.'

'Go and tell your Dad I'm ready to go to the Esplanade now,' Gran said, as soon as they were out of Mr Baldock's yard. 'Now I've come this far, I might as well go on up the hill. Linda will look after me. Oh, bring my bag, will you? It's on the table by the window. There's something in it I might need.'

When they reached the house on the Esplanade, a woman from the one of the flats in the house next door was just coming out of the gate.

'I can't get any answer,' she said, looking troubled. 'I've been knocking and knocking. I don't suppose you know where Miss Marchbanks is staying, do you? I think she ought to be told.'

'Told what?' Gran asked, sharply.

'Why, about Miss Tregoran ... Oh, don't you know? I thought that was why you'd come...'

'What about her?' asked Gran. 'I thought she was in a nursing home.'

'That's just it,' said the neighbour, 'she isn't. She went off all right on Friday afternoon – Sea Haven, it is, at the end of the Esplanade. The builders are coming next week and Miss Tregoran didn't want to be here when they started knocking the old place about and Miss Marchbanks went off to London for the week-end on Saturday morning. Sometime on Saturday afternoon Miss Tregoran disappeared. Nobody quite knows when, but later in the evening one of the old ladies remembered Miss Tregoran telling her she was going home. Somebody came down, of course, but they couldn't make anybody hear. They tried ringing but she doesn't hear the 'phone now. Two of the nurses have been this morning and I've been knocking on and off, but we can't get an answer. I was wondering if I ought to ring the police. I mean, if she's had an accident...'

'We'll see to it,' said Angie's father. 'Come on, Gran. Come on, girls. Let's see if we can make the old lady hear us. If not...'

He was a nice man. He had no idea why Gran had wanted so badly to be brought to the house on the Esplanade, but if she had had a premonition about her precious Miss Lucy and something really was wrong, he was prepared to do anything he could to help.

'Never mind knocking on the front door,' Gran said as they went down the drive. 'Go round the back. I've got a key of the garden door.'

She took a big iron key from her bag and held it up. 'Me and Bessie and Phipps used to take this out with us on our evening off, so we could come in late without waking Cook. Her room was in the basement.'

'Gran!' said Angie's father. 'That was donkey's years ago! There'll have been new locks put on since then.'

'I don't see why,' Gran said, going briskly up the steps to the garden door. 'It looks just the same to me.'

'Do you think we ought ...?' began Angie's father as Gran put the key in the lock.

'There's no "ought" about it,' Gran said firmly. 'I'm going in. You do what you like.'

The key turned easily in the ancient lock. Gran opened the door.

Linda had the feeling of stepping back in time. She saw the long passage leading to the front hall, the big front door with its stained glass, the two flights of narrow back stairs, one going down to the basement kitchen, and one going up to the nursery and the attic bedroom that Elsie and Bessie had shared. It was all just as Gran had described. Even the wallpaper seemed old-fashioned.

Gran had gone down to the front hall. She stood at the foot of the wide staircase and called 'Miss Lucy – Are you there, Miss Lucy?'

A door in the hall opened. Linda's heart missed a beat. Miss Lucy? A little girl, with a pale face and blue eyes and long fair hair . . .? Or a strange, unnatural creature with Miss Lucy's hair and Miss Dupont's dark, cruel face?

A quavering voice asked, 'Janet? Is that you?' and a little frail old lady with silvery hair appeared in the doorway, peering short-sightedly at Gran.

'No, Miss Lucy,' Gran said, gently. 'It's me – Elsie. Are you all right?'

'Oh, Elsie!' said the old lady, tremulously. 'I have such a headache! I had that dreadful dream again. I haven't had it for years . . . I dreamed I was a doll . . .'

Linda felt her stomach give a sickening lurch. She caught Gran's eye. Gran looked very grim.

If Miss Lucy was no longer a doll, then who was?

CHAPTER TEN

... And Tide

'I only came back for my reading glasses,' Miss Lucy said. 'Janot forgot to pack them for me. They were by my chair in the drawing room. I just sat down for a minute ... I was a little tired, you see, walking in that heat. I must have gone to sleep. I woke up when I heard you calling me ... and with such a headache.'

They took her back to the nursing home a little bemused at having lost a day. Angie's father said he would bring Gran up again later so she and Miss Lucy could sit and chat about old times.

Back in Quay Street, Linda went at once to Joanna's house.

Samantha opened the door to her, obviously about to go out. She was wearing the sun-hat Tilda had borrowed, but without the blue ribbon.

'She's not back,' she said, 'and I haven't heard a word from her. I think she might have 'phoned. I suppose she's gone with that creepy friend of hers, back to *her* house, wherever that is. We certainly don't want her here again in a hurry. I suppose she was mad at me for borrowing her beastly beads, but she didn't have to try and kill me for *that* ... Oh, help.' She put her hand to her forehead in a dramatic gesture. 'I've still got her necklace! It's in my purse. I had to take it off last night, it wouldn't stay in my hair. Kept slipping down and flapping about. You don't know where she lives do you? I'd hate anyone to think I'd pinched it.'

'As a matter of fact,' said Linda, scarcely able to keep the jubilation out of her voice, 'It doesn't belong to Tilda. It belongs to Miss Tregoran. She lives on the Esplanade.'

'Ah!' cried Samantha, 'I thought those pearls were too good to belong to a kid like that. *Borrowed* it, did she? I suppose that's why she and Jo went up there yesterday evening, to try and put it back before Miss What's-her-name found out ...'

She opened her purse and took out the necklace, dangling it in front of Linda.

'Look, since you seem to know who it belongs to, maybe you'd like to take it back? I'd do it myself, only I'm supposed to be going to Emma's for lunch ...'

Hardly able to believe her luck, Linda held out her cupped hands. Samantha let go of the necklace. It slid into Linda's hands, coiling itself softly into a little shimmering heap of perfectly matched pearls.

'Thanks,' said Samantha. 'Must go now. What was it you wanted, anyway? Just to see if Jo was back?'

'No,' said Linda, 'I mean, yes ... but I wanted to ask her if I could have my workbag back. I left it in her room yesterday afternoon.'

'Oh, well, go up and get it then,' Samantha said. 'I *must* go. Give the front door a good bang when you come out. It doesn't shut properly if you don't.'

So that's why the Stones always slam the door, thought Linda, as she ran up the stairs. With a dry mouth and a tight feeling in her chest she peeped into Joanna's room. It wasn't simply the old workbag she had come to find. The room was neat and tidy. There was nothing out of place – and no small doll lay on the carefully made bed.

Linda went across the landing to the room she knew Tilda had used. Very gently she pushed open the door, her heart thumping. The bed in here, too, had been made, but on it lay the embroidered workbag, its contents spilled across the counterpane.

Linda began to collect them up, pushing them

roughly into the bag. Halfway through she stopped. The brush was missing. Then she saw, on the dark green bedcover, a few tiny scraps of thin white material and some snippets of Joanna's bright red hair.

'But she can't make a wig out of Joanna's hair!' protested Angie. 'It's too short. Anyway, she'd look even worse with red hair than she did with Miss Lucy's.'

'Joanna is young and strong,' Gran said gravely. 'Miss Lucy is old and frail. She never was very robust and she was very ill earlier in the year.'

'*That's* why Tilda couldn't walk far without stopping!' said Linda. 'Yes, I can see why she'd want a new wig – any new wig – but how could she make the change-over? Wouldn't she turn back into a doll when Miss Lucy's wig was taken off?'

'She'd have to persuade Joanna to put the new wig on for her,' Gran admitted.

'She's daft enough,' sniffed Angie. 'She wouldn't know what was going to happen to her of course,' she added.

'She'd have been mesmerized … hypnotized. Told what to do and she'd have done it without question,' Gran said. 'That's what happened to Miss Lucy. That's how she was able to learn so much in such a short time. Everybody thought Miss Dupont's methods were wonderful . . . but Dr Charlton guessed what was happening, though, of course, it wasn't really Miss Lucy he saw. Dr Marchbanks wouldn't listen, though. He thought he'd made a great discovery in Miss Lucy's new governess.'

'So he had,' said Angie. 'She was a witch.'

As soon as they decently could after Sunday lunch, the two girls set off to look for Tilda. 'They've been back,' Mrs Porter said, hearing them knocking on Joanna's door, 'but I think they've gone again. I heard the door slam, not five minutes ago. I was going to call them in for lunch, but they didn't give me time.' Linda and Angie walked up the hill to the castle, where a little trickle of tourists was moving towards the gate. Linda searched among them for a red-haired childish figure, but there wasn't one.

'Why do you think she went back?' asked Angie.

'For the necklace, perhaps,' said Linda.

In the town they caught sight of red hair twice, but nothing like Joanna's.

They wandered about aimlessly for a couple of hours, getting hotter and hotter and more fed up.

'She *must* still be in the town *somewhere*,' Linda said.

'Let's try the station,' Angie suggested. 'Wasn't she supposed to be going to London when she was here before? There aren't many trains on a Sunday.'

'She hasn't got any money,' Linda said, 'and I don't suppose Jo had all that much. Not enough to get her very far, anyway. Still, it's worth a try.'

The station was almost deserted.

They went into the Booking Office and the Ladies' Cloakroom and looked along the empty platform. Then they hung about outside for a bit. At last Angie said, 'Let's go home. I'm getting cold now.'

It was much cooler than it had been earlier. The sky had clouded over and a chill wind had sprung up.

'She might try to get back to France, I suppose,' Linda said, some time after tea. 'I can't imagine how, though.'

'Boat,' said Angie.

'Of course!' cried Linda. 'Come on . . .'

They were running down Quay Street. The sun had disappeared completely now and the wind was stronger.

Linda looked up at the leaden sky.

'I think there's going to be a storm,' she said. 'We should have brought our raincoats.'

The tide was on the turn. Boats were bobbing on the sullen sea, little knots of people stood about, watching a few boatmen making ready to go out.

Anxiously Linda and Angie searched among them, looking for a dark, unlovely face, or a mop of bright red hair.

Then they saw her, walking along the stone jetty, a small figure wearing jeans and a T-shirt.

'It's Jo!' cried Linda, joyfully. 'She didn't put the red wig on Tilda after all. She just took Miss Lucy's off.' She started to run, calling excitedly, 'Joanna ... wait! Joanna.'

The wind was stronger now. It buffeted Linda as she ran. She could hear Angie behind her, shouting, 'No, Linda! Come back!'

Linda shouted again. 'Joanna!' The hurrying figure in front of her was nearing the end of the jetty now. It was a stupid and dangerous thing to do, to stand near the edge of the jetty in this wind. What was wrong with Joanna? Was she still under Tilda's spell?

As she struggled nearer to her, Linda could see that Joanna was carrying something in her right hand. A doll! A wooden doll!

She was right at the end of the jetty. A gust of wind made her stagger.

'Jo!' Linda cried, desperately.

The figure turned – and she was not Joanna. There was a malevolent smile on the thin lips, malice and triumph in the dark, glittering eyes. She raised her arm and flung the doll that was Joanna into the cold, angry sea.

Linda screamed, hardly able to keep her balance in the raging wind. Behind her, Angie was still shouting. Other voices had joined in, calling to her, and the unspeakable creature ahead of her, to come back.

A gust of wind, more violent than any before, spun Linda round. She did not see the hastily-made, ill-fitting red wig being whipped off the head of the doll-child, but she heard the small clatter of the second wooden doll as it hit the edge of the jetty before it, too, fell into the water.

Gasping and spluttering, Joanna struggled in the wind-whipped sea, surprised to find herself there. Instinct made her start to swim towards the jetty, though she had no clear idea where she was. There were shouts from the shore, an engine started up and a little speed-boat zoomed towards her. As she was being hauled aboard she saw Linda, on her knees on the edge of the jetty, peering down at her with frightened eyes.

'We heard at the station that a child had been blown off the jetty,' Mrs Stone said. 'Some holiday-makers, on their way home, saw it happen. It never occurred to us it might be you. Whatever were you doing there?'

Joanna, looking pink and cheerful after a warm bath and a hot drink, was sitting up in bed wrapped in an eiderdown.

Her mother hugged her and then gave a cry of astonishment.

'Jo! Whatever's happened to your hair? It's all hacked to bits at the back!'

Joanna frowned and put up her hand to feel the untidy mess at the back of her head.

'How did that happen?' she asked, surprised.

'It was your precious Tilda, I bet,' said Samantha. 'I told you she was mad!'

'Tilda?' said Joanna, vaguely. 'I don't remember...' She yawned.

'Let her sleep now,' Mrs Stone said, bustling Samantha out of the room.

Later, when Linda and Angie called to see how Joanna was, she said, 'I really feel as though I ought to do something about this dreadful child

Jo had here for the weekend. I've been hearing the most terrible tales about her. She sounds positively dangerous. Do you know, she searched Sam's room this afternoon while Sam was out! I don't know what Jo was thinking about, to let her. I really feel I ought to tell her parents.'

'She doesn't live here,' Linda said, hastily.

'Oh, a *visitor*,' said Mrs Stone, as though that explained everything. 'Even so, is she staying somewhere on the Esplanade? Samantha said something about a pearl necklace belonging to somebody up there...'

'She wasn't staying there this time,' Linda said, truthfully. 'Anyway, she's gone now. She went this evening.'

'Back to the funny farm, I suppose,' grinned Samantha.

'She left a ghastly green dress in Joanna's wardrobe,' Mrs Stone said. 'And a pair of button boots. Boots! I ask you ... Still, if she's gone, there's not much we can do about it, is there.'

'I was afraid she was going to start asking a lot of questions,' Linda said, as they walked back. 'Luckily Samantha hadn't remembered Miss Lucy's name. Gran said it was in the local papers about Miss Dupont going off and not coming back, and Mrs Marchbanks's pearls disappearing.

There might be people Mrs Stone knows who still remember . . .'

'How are we going to get the necklace back to Miss Lucy?'

'Gran said she'd take it back, but then she said it would look as though she was the one who stole it, so I said we could say it was in the workbag Mr Baldock gave me.'

'Well, it was, wasn't it? Round the doll's neck.'

Linda laughed. 'So it was! I'd forgotten that.'

'You're not the only one forgetting things,' Angie said. 'Joanna seems to have forgotten quite a lot.'

'Best thing,' said Linda. She shivered.'I never want to live through another weekend like this one. It's been like a bad dream. I wish to goodness I'd never looked inside that beastly bag. I don't think Mr Baldock would have given it to me if he hadn't thought I wanted it . . .'

'Chuck it away,' Angie advised.

'I think I will,' said Linda – and added, 'I wonder what happened to the hairbrush?'

But that was a question which couldn't be answered.

In a little fishing village on the coast of Brittany, a thin silent woman sat on an old wooden bench, staring out to sea. She had lived in the village as long as anyone could remember, though no one knew how she had come there, or when. She earned her living in whatever way she could – as a dressmaker, a laundrymaid, a cleaner, a servant. Anything anyone wanted done she would do, if she could, without question or argument. She was quiet and biddable and completely reliable. Her ageless, changeless face was known to everyone, young and old alike. She was an oddity. They called her 'La Muette', the dumb one, though the name on her passport was Clothilde Dupont.

She sat as she had sat many, many times before, watching and waiting, till the dusk came and one after another the lights went on in the little houses behind her. Someone came out, as someone always did, to say to her, 'Time to go home, Clothilde,' and, obediently, she went back to her lodging.

Across the water, as the twilight deepened into night, the lights came on in the little seaside town that had given her life. Far out to sea, floating face downwards in the fast-running tide, a little wooden doll, dressed in jeans and a T-shirt, was being carried inexorably towards the coast of France.